# PREPARE FOR ACTION

## John Creasey

Master crime fiction writer John Creasey's 562 titles (or so) have sold more than 80 million copies in over 25 languages. After enduring 743 rejection slips, the young Creasey's career was kickstarted by winning a newspaper writing competition. He went on to collect multiple honours from The Mystery Writers of America including the Edgar Award for best novel in 1962 and the coveted title of Grand Master in 1969. Creasey's prolific output included 11 different series including Roger West, the Toff, the Baron, Patrick Dawlish, Gideon, Dr Palfrey, and Department Z, published both under his own name and 10 other pseudonyms.

Creasey was born in Surrey in 1908 and, when not travelling extensively, lived between Bournemouth and Salisbury for most of his life. He died in England in 1973.

## The Department Z Series

# PREPARE FOR ACTION

*Department Z*

JOHN CREASEY

ipso books

This edition published in 2017 by Ipso Books

First published by John Long Limited 1942, revised by Arrow in 1966

Ipso Books is a division of Peters Fraser + Dunlop Ltd

Drury House, 34-43 Russell Street, London WC2B 5HA

# Chapter 1
# A Cousin Has Charm

There was little doubt that Sir Edmund Quayle was frightened; his plump face and little blue eyes betrayed it, although he tried hard to hide the fact from Mr. Gregory Hanton, who liked to be known as Hanton of Heath Place.

'My dear Hanton, I can't be satisfied with that, it's preposterous,' declared Quayle. 'If Brent did know that we worked together, if he even so much as suspected it and put his suspicions on paper, think of what would happen to me! And I am positive that I am being watched. I no longer feel safe. You must be aware of the tremendous risk I take every time I send information along to you.'

As he drained a whisky-and-soda he peered anxiously at the short, bald-headed figure of Hanton of Heath Place. That gentleman, who was wealthy enough to want more money, and had long since sold his soul in its pursuit, pursed his full lips and regarded Quayle without favour.

'I know, I know,' said Hanton testily. 'You're on the spot and I'm sitting pretty. That's what *you* think.' He lit a cigarette and broke the match in two, eyeing Quayle all the time. 'But you're right one way,' he admitted at length. 'We'll have to see Brent's papers again. We may have missed something last year. Listen, Quayle, I'm going to be clever. I'll fix it with Lannigan, he can get the dirty work done.'

'I strongly suggest you don't do that! Lannigan doesn't know I'm in it, and he mustn't learn! Find a man who won't talk.'

'Maybe you're right. I'll get it done. You watch your step, and don't contact me any more until it's over. Is that clear?'

Furtively Quayle left Heath Place, near the Somerset village of Lashley, between Bath and Radstock. Hanton watched from a window; so did another man from the end of the drive; both agreed, shortly afterwards, that Sir Edmund had not been followed.

A boom of thunder rumbled, and soon afterwards the dark clouds were split in two by a jagged flash of lightning, which was too far from the bank of the stream and the two men resting near it to affect either light or shadow.

Both men were large. Both were dressed in flannels and tweed jackets, light blue shirts and Old Carthusian ties. Moreover, both were smoking pipes of the same pattern.

No stranger passing them could have distinguished one from the other. Friends and acquaintances knew that Mark Errol's hair was, perhaps, a little darker and a little less tidy than Michael's, his cousin, that Mike's eyes were grey flecked with blue, and Mark's flecked with green, but the difference was clear only to those who looked closely at them.

For many years their world had considered these two men inseparable, and certainly they were fast friends, sharing a flat in London and a cottage near the stream where they were now sitting.

Together they had 'enlisted' in the service of Department Z, an Intelligence Department which made great calls upon them. Perhaps the greatest was that from time to time it entailed their separation, but ten days before, when they had returned from Spain on a mission of considerable importance, Gordon Craigie, their Chief, had dispensed his blessings, told them that they looked worn out, and sent them to their cottage for a rest.

'All being well,' he had said, 'you can have a couple of weeks, and I'll make it longer if I can.'

Another roll of thunder broke much nearer, and this time the flash of lightning preceding it brightened the darkening countryside ominously. The clouds were almost above their heads.

'We'd better be moving,' said Mike.

They walked briskly towards a small copse near the stream, passing through it before reaching the cottage. It was neither particularly old nor picturesque, but the half-acre of garden surrounding it was a sight worth seeing, the front blazing with flowers set against a velvet lawn, the back heavy with crops.

A few spots of rain were falling as the Errols reached the front door. Inside, a flurry of white told them that one of their domestic helpers was there, preparing the evening meal. They had been walking since tea, after spending much of the morning and afternoon on Old Totton's farm.

Once in the narrow porch, Mike said abruptly: 'Hello, there's some post.'

'Craigie?' Mark put a great deal of expression into the name.

'It doesn't look like it.' Mike picked up an envelope from a table near the door, and Mark stared at it over his

3

shoulder. 'It can't be anything interesting, anyhow, or it wouldn't be addressed to both of us. I'll put the light on.'

The room was in shadow, darkened by the gathering storm. Its low ceiling, crossed in places with oak beams, forced Mike to duck low as he stepped to the light switches, put by some ingenious country electrician as far away from the front door as was inconveniently possible. A clatter of crockery came from the kitchen, but neither the clatter nor another flash of lightning followed by a torrent of rain and a blare of thunder distracted Mike's attention from the letter.

Neither cousin had looked towards the far corner of the lounge-dining-room, nor seen anyone sitting there. But as Mark slit open the envelope someone stirred. Both men were unaware of it, and Mike said, 'It couldn't be from Aunt Bess, could it?'

'In fifteen seconds I'll tell you,' said Mark, unfolding the letter.

'I can tell you sooner than that, that it isn't,' said a girl from the corner. 'It's from me.'

Both men started, and turned swiftly about.

The electric light revealed the girl. She was tall, and dressed in tweeds, her hat pulled down a little over one eye, Tyrolean fashion, and with a feather sticking from it.

'Good evening,' said Mark, recovering himself quickly.

'How do you do,' said Mike, not to be outdone.

'I'm very well, thank you,' said the girl. She was smiling a little, and they liked her voice.

'You might have addressed it to me,' said Mike reproachfully.

'If you'll be quiet a minute,' said Mark testily, 'I'll read the letter. That'll save a lot of talk and explanation.'

Mike scanned it over Mark's shoulder, conscious of the steady and rather amused gaze from the girl.

The letter began, rather unexpectedly, *Dear Mark and Michael.* It went on:

> *Coming out of the blue like this, you'll be surprised to hear from me. It is a long time since we saw one another, and you may not even remember 'Gina' with a 'G' as in 'George'—or does it strike a chord?*
>
> *Whether or no, I shall be in Guildford on Thursday, and Aunt Bess tells me that you're not far away from there, so I am going to call for an hour or two on Thursday evening.*
>
> *If you haven't remembered 'Gina' yet, think of the story of the two goldfish we couldn't divide into three! Oh, yes, three cousins.*
>
> 

*Yours,*
*Regina Brent.*

'Gina!' exclaimed Mike, swinging round with outstretched arms. 'Gina, you in the flesh!' He gripped her hands. 'Three shares of two goldfish—oh, my hat, how many years does that take us back?'

'Idiot, where's your tact?' demanded Mark. 'Not many.' He too approached, and when Mike freed her hands calmly took her right one, drew her nearer, and kissed her right cheek. 'Cousinly salutations, Gina,' he said gravely. 'Mike isn't himself, you've gathered that, or he wouldn't have forgotten that cousins can kiss.'

He smiled as he stared into her laughing eyes.

A flash of lightning and another clap of thunder made him start, but not look away from her. Nor did Mike shift his gaze, but allowed Mark's provocative sally to go unchallenged.

'How long can you stay?' he demanded quickly. 'An hour or two just isn't good enough. We're on holiday, you'll have to see that out.'

'We'll get a week's extension,' declared Mark. 'I——'

He stopped abruptly, and his expression altered. So did Mike's.

It was not surprising, for the laughter had gone from the girl's eyes. The change was remarkable; a few seconds before she had been bubbling over with good spirits, but something had happened, something which saddened her. Both cousins realised it, both sought for an explanation; and Mark saw a possibility.

'Gina,' he said quietly. 'The family's all right?'

Regina stepped back, and sat on the edge of a chair. The room was very still, except for the beating of the rain against the windows. The next roll of thunder was farther away, but it produced a heavy, sonorous background to her quiet:

'No. Mum and Dad are dead.'

'Good lord!' said Mike, and crushed out his cigarette. 'I wish—I mean——'

Regina said quickly: 'Look here, we're starting off on the wrong foot. They've been dead over twelve months now, and—well, I'm over the shock and it's surprising how often I don't think of them.' She paused, and then went on: 'I suppose it was remembering you two, and the old house, and everything that went with it, but I shouldn't have introduced the subject that way. A year *is* a long time,' she added quietly.

'Ye-es,' agreed Mike. 'All the same, I think I know how you feel. I'd no idea.'

'We should have kept in touch,' said Mark abruptly.

'My coming here is not entirely an accident, or because I was near Guildford.' She hesitated, aware that they were puzzled by her words. The gaiety in her manner, which had been so apparent when she first appeared, had faded, and they knew that she was still thinking of her parents. They remembered, too, that Regina had been an only child, and adored by Alice and James Brent.

Mike, at thirty-six, calculated that she must be thirty. No, twenty-eight or nine. He couldn't be sure which, but in any case she would pass for twenty-five.

Mike said, 'Did you say you didn't come altogether by accident, Gina?'

'Yes,' admitted Regina. She hesitated, and then said: 'It's all rather fantastic, Mike and Mark, and you'll probably laugh at me. But something queer happened, and Aunt Bess said you two might be able to help.'

'If we can——' began Mike.

'We will,' finished Mark. 'Let's have the story, Gina.'

# CHAPTER 2
# REGINA'S STORY

For some seconds Regina Brent sat without speaking, marshalling her thoughts.

'It starts with Father's death,' she said abruptly.

That startled them, although they made no comment, and after a noticeable pause she went on:

'I say that, although they were killed together in a motor accident, just over a year ago. Dad had been working extremely hard, and needed a change, and I was to join them at Looe for a few days. We'd been looking forward to it for weeks, and—well, there it was. At the time I didn't dream that it might have been more than an accident.' She paused again, turning to look at the cousins. The two faces, so much alike, were regarding her with close interest, and she went on hurriedly: 'I'd been working in Westmorland with a family Dad knew, but after that I left the job and joined the A.T.S.'

Involuntarily, Mike glanced at her clothes.

'I'm on leave,' said Regina quickly. 'Nine more whole days! The thing is, you should know that Dad was doing a lot of work with the Ministry of Economic Warfare. Before the war, of course, he was always on the Continent.'

The Errols knew that James Brent had been the managing director of a firm of manufacturers with a large trade.

Regina went on: 'I don't know what he was doing, but there was a lot of anxious searching, after he died, for his papers—he had taken some work home with him. The papers were found near the scene of the crash, two or three days afterwards, so the excitement died down. I didn't think anything of it at the time, but since I found this diary I've wondered about it.'

Mike said: 'You've wondered whether the papers were taken away and returned afterwards.'

Regina stared at him.

'Does it strike you like that, too?' She sounded incredulous. A pause, and then she continued: 'The thing that really worries me is the diary. I didn't know he kept one, but I was going through some papers of his last week—in an old box I've been meaning to turn out for a long time, but I just couldn't bring my mind to it—and came across it.' She hesitated for a moment before saying sharply: 'Oh, I expect I'm dreaming, but several things in the diary suggested that he was—well, frightened of being attacked.'

'Have you got it with you?' asked Mark.

'Yes,' said Regina. She put a hand to a hip pocket in her skirt, and drew out a slim diary, about three inches by two in size. She held it tightly for a moment and said: 'Mark—and you, Mike. If you think I'm just working myself into hysteria about it, you'll say so, won't you?'

'Of course,' said Mark, and stretched out his hand for the diary.

They were both so intent on Regina and the story that they noticed nothing outside. Had they glanced out then they would have glimpsed a man who had stepped cautiously from some bushes and reached the cover of the house. As it was, Mark opened the diary, unaware of the nearness of the stranger, who, sidling along the outer wall, was drawing nearer to the window. His right hand was outstretched, his left was in his pocket, the elbow crooked as if he were ready to draw the hand out swiftly.

A tall thin man, he was dressed in dark grey, a Homburg hat pulled well down over his eyes.

'Turn to the June entries first,' said Regina.

Mark let the pages of the diary flutter over. Outside, a rustling breeze stirred trees and flowers, and made one of the curtains blow against the open window. The breeze turned the pages of the diary also, and Mark glanced round, a hand outstretched to push the window to. Mike did the same.

The sound following was sharp and abrupt. Fast upon it, Mike and Mark jumped to their feet, Mark a foot ahead of his cousin.

They could see Mrs. Gee, the housekeeper, standing on the garden path, staring towards the window. Obviously she had screamed. The shadow of the man nearby was on the path immediately beneath them. Mark saw it move, and saw the added shadow of a gun appear. He tossed the diary over his shoulder, and it landed on a chair. Then he put one foot on the window ledge and jumped out.

There was the sharp crack of a revolver shot. Mike heard it, and also heard his cousin grunt. Mark fell with his hands in front of him. The assailant jumped backwards while Mike leapt forward, throwing himself through the air in an endeavour to crush the man downwards and prevent him from shooting.

His right hand swept outwards, striking the other's outstretched arm. His fist knocked the gun flying from long fingers, as he hurtled to the ground.

The man in grey took to his heels, reached a shrubbery and dived into it, and Mike waited only long enough to retrieve the automatic before following, guided by the sound of the other's progress.

While crashing through the tightly interlaced boughs, he caught no glimpse of his quarry, and he remembered that beyond the shrubs there was a footpath leading to the river in one direction, and the nearest road in the other. He judged that the man would turn to the road.

He swung right, hoping to cut him off, and soon reached the footpath, breathing hard but careful to keep out of sight in case the other had a second gun. Then he heard footsteps running in the opposite direction, and, venturing forward, caught a glimpse of his man racing towards the river.

The footpath led amongst the trees, and the man was lost to sight a moment afterwards. Mike started in pursuit, but was no more than halfway to the river when he stubbed his foot against an exposed root. He pitched forward, striking the ground heavily. Cursing, he picked himself up, but his ankle buckled under him, and he knew it would be useless to continue the chase.

The running footsteps seemed a long way off.

The ambulance arrived.

Mike sat and watched Mark being placed on a stretcher. The doctor who had come with the ambulance had glanced at the bandaging Regina had applied to his ankle and announced satisfaction with it. He told Mike that the operating theatre would be ready as soon as the patient reached the hospital, and that no time would be lost.

Mike felt an odd sense of deflation when Mark had gone. The doctor told him that he would telephone the moment the operation was over, and that there was no point in going into Guildford. Mike felt that was so, for the time being at least.

He looked at Regina.

She was sitting in a chair opposite him, and fingering the diary which Mike had thrown over his shoulder. She glanced down at the pages, then at Mike. He saw her eyes fill with tears as she turned her face away,

'Oh Mike, I'm so *damned* sorry I caused this!'

Mike stared at her, amazed. 'You caused it? What on earth gave you that idea?'

'Don't you understand, they wanted the diary!' Regina almost shouted the words. 'They must have followed me. I half thought I was being followed yesterday, and in London I've been haunted by them!'

Five days before, on the start of fourteen days' leave, she had gone to Aunt Bess, who lived in Somerset. The personal oddments of her father and mother, collected in two boxes, had needed sorting out for some time, and she had started on the task. Before doing so she had heard in great detail from Aunt Bess (her mother's sister) of an attempted burglary at the Somerset house. It had been a nine days' wonder in the village, and Gina had grown tired of hearing about it, until she had discovered that an attempt had been made to force the lock of her father's box.

'I wondered if the box had been the purpose of the robbery,' went on Regina. 'The suspicion didn't really sink in, but I *did* wonder. Then I cleared it out, and the next evening I was glancing through the diary and read the bits that—that suggested Dad had been frightened of an attack on his life. I told Aunt Bess about it, and she suggested that

I came to see you. She seems to think you're something to do with the police. She read about you in the paper—she actually had some cuttings. *Are* you in the police force?'

'Some might say so, in a manner of speaking. We're acquainted, anyhow.'

Regina appeared satisfied with that, and went on: 'I telephoned your flat, but there was no answer, so I wrote to you, hoping you'd get the letter in time. When I called at the flat the caretaker told me where you were, and said he'd re-addressed the letter. I wrote again, that's the letter you have now, and came down here. But—oh, I suppose I was dreaming, but I seemed to be followed and watched everywhere. It *must* have been imagination.'

'Must?' asked Mike. He was intrigued, and for the first time felt an easing of the weight of anxiety about Mark. 'I wouldn't say so, Gina. If you were followed for that diary—have you read it anywhere but at Aunt Bess's?'

Regina said: 'I looked at it in the train. And, Mike——'

'Yes?' he said as she paused.

'Someone stole my handbag. I had the diary in my pocket, and most of my money in a case, so it didn't matter, but it made me even more sure that I was followed.'

'Ye-es,' said Mike slowly. 'And that someone's after the diary. I wonder why?' He stretched forward and took it from her fingers, remembering that she had advised Mark to look in the entries for June. Before he read a line, the telephone rang.

Regina answered it.

'Hold on a moment.' She looked at Mike. 'It's a man named Loftus—do you want to speak to him?'

'Loftus!' exclaimed Mike. 'Do I want——' he jumped up, then winced again and stopped speaking abruptly. His eyes were brighter, and there was an eager expression on his face. 'Yes, I do,' he said. 'If I'm a policeman, Loftus is my Assistant Commissioner.' He limped to the telephone, and stood with his weight on his sound leg, and said: 'Mike here, Bill, and I've got something for you before you start.'

'Forget it,' said Loftus heartily. 'I've a job for the two of you, and it's urgent. Pack up and say goodbye to the country, and come up here right away, will you?'

# Chapter 3
# Regina Meets Others

There was a short pause, while Regina regarded Mike's set, strained face, and wondered what had been said to him. Mike remained silent until Loftus spoke again in a steadier voice.

'What's the trouble, Mike?'

Mike drew a deep breath.

'More than odds and ends,' he said. 'We've had bother, and Mark's taken a bullet in his chest. I don't know whether it's one of our shows or not.'

'That's bad,' said Loftus, his voice no longer hearty, but quiet and sincere. 'How is he?'

'I'll know in an hour, I hope.'

'Ring me back when there's word,' said Loftus. 'I'll get someone else busy on the job I had in mind. Are you on your own?'

'I'm with a cousin,' said Mike. 'A long-lost cousin. I'm all right, if that's what you mean.'

'That's what I meant,' Loftus assured him. 'All right, Mike. Ring me as soon as you can.'

Mike limped to his chair and lowered himself cautiously, then lit a cigarette.

'Now about that diary,' he said.

Regina sat on the arm of his chair. He read the four entries in the year-old diary quickly at first, with Regina following the words over his shoulder. The entries were brief and concise, written in a small, even hand not unlike that on the envelope he had picked up from the table in the room.

*I have not reported an accident which happened this afternoon, but think that I should. At all events, I must watch carefully.*

*Q. laughed at my fancies this afternoon. I wish I disliked the man less. He pooh-poohs my fears, and tells me that I need a holiday. That, at least, is right.*

*Only four days to go, thank heavens. The strain is really worrying me. I don't think Alice has any idea of what is troubling me. I had a sharp exchange of words with Q. again today. It is quite obvious that I shall have to ask for a transfer. I cannot work with the man any longer.*

*I have never looked forward to a holiday so much as I am doing this one. Q. asked me to postpone it for a few days, but I refused point-blank. I wish that I could believe all the trouble is due to my imagination, all the same. What conceivable reason could anyone have in killing me?*

Mike finished reading, but went through each entry again before putting the diary aside and glancing into Regina's eyes. She was frowning as she said: 'He was overworked, Mike. Two doctors told him that he would break down unless he got away for a few weeks.' She paused, and when Mike did not answer, added abruptly: 'Was he imagining trouble because he had overworked?'

'If you go on like this you'll be a candidate for collapse, too,' said Mike quietly. 'If his brain was working on a note of hysteria, he had the coolest and calmest way of making a record of it that I can imagine. Is there anything else in the diary?'

'Nothing that has anything to do with this.' said Regina. 'The early part is just a list of appointments that he kept, and notes of what arrangements he made. It isn't until the last few pages that he makes any comments like those you've read. You'll want to keep the diary, I suppose?'

'Ye-es.' Mike rubbed his nose. 'I wonder if the visitor tonight wanted to get it? Where are the other things that were in that box?'

'Still in it. I just tidied it up and locked it again.'

'Good. The first job is to make sure that nothing can be taken from it until we've had another look,' said Mike briskly. 'The second is to send the diary to Loftus and Craigie—you'll meet them soon—and have them check it thoroughly. The third is to make inquiries about "Q".' He looked at her inquiringly.

' "Q" stands for Quayle,' she told him.

'And Quayle was his immediate chief, I take it?'

'Yes and no,' said Regina. 'They had the same authority in the office. Dad handled the personnel, Quayle looked after details and general correspondence. I don't know much about it. It was all hush-hush, and Dad would never talk about his work, even before the war.'

'Quayle—Quayle—I've heard the name somewhere. He——' Mike paused abruptly, and then snapped his fingers. 'Sir Edmund Quayle, of course! He's just been sued for libel by one of his assistants. Is that the man?'

'That's the man,' said Regina. 'I didn't know him well, but he was one of those cold people. Fishy, smooth—you know what I mean.'

'Yes,' said Mike. 'I'll have to meet him some day.' He stubbed out his cigarette, and was staring at her when the telephone rang again. He started, but Regina told him to keep still while she went to take the message. He waited in a ferment of anxiety until she said:

'I'm speaking for him ... yes ... oh, thank God! When ... yes, I'll tell him, thank you.' She turned to face Mike, her eyes shining. 'It's successful, and he'll be all right!'

'Thank God for that,' echoed Mike fervently. 'Gina, we're free to get cracking. London for us, while there's time and daylight left. We'll stay at the Cumberworth for the night, and get down to Somerset in the morning. Travel light, and don't be surprised at our speed,' he added, ten times more lighthearted than he had been before the telephone call.

His excitement, born of relief, dimmed somewhat in the next two hours. By that time they were approaching Whitehall, and many things had happened.

First, he had telephoned Loftus to make the appointment and report. Then he had received a visit from Inspector Lee of Guildford, who apologised because he had been detained. Lee was an oldish man, who told Mike that he had been instructed to act at all times on any suggestions from the Errols. (That was common with all the Department Z agents, ensuring quick police cooperation in emergency.) Lee regretted that there was no trace of the man whose description Regina had telephoned, and expressed the hope that Mr. Errol would make an official report, which he could present to his Chief Constable, on the matter of the attack.

Mike had done so, briefly.

By then, Regina had been ready. Soon afterwards they had called at her Guildford hotel and collected her one case, and started for London. Driving a Lagonda, Mike had travelled at considerable speed, not affected by his sprained ankle, and neither of them had talked a great deal.

Mike turned the car into Brook Street.

He had arranged to see Loftus and Craigie there, and to do the necessary talking, instead of going to the Department's office in Whitehall. For his own part he was quite sure of Regina, but Craigie and Loftus would wonder whether she was all she pretended to be—he could almost see them wondering—and consequently Loftus had preferred not to allow a stranger into the office. On such simple precautions rested much of the success of the Department, and that success was considerable.

Mike pulled into the kerb, and Regina said quietly: 'What kind of man am I going to meet, Mike?'

'We-ell,' Mike said slowly, 'it's difficult to put Bill Loftus into a few words. You'll like him. A big fellow, who lost a leg in a shindy a year or so ago. He's second-in-command to Gordon Craigie, who'll probably be here as well. You won't take to Gordon on sight. Thin, rather dry, distant kind of cove until you get to know him. He'll probably give you the impression that he doesn't believe half of what you're saying.'

During the telling both Loftus and Craigie listened without interrupting. Regina noticed nothing, but Mike caught the impression that between them there was a constraint which he found hard to understand. He finished the narrative and then handed the diary over, saying:

'So it looks to me as if the quicker we have that box looked after, the better.'

'H'm,' said Loftus, and glanced down at the diary. 'This is a queer turn-up. Shall I tell them?' He looked at Craigie, and received a nod. For a moment he hesitated, as if deliberately increasing the tension, and then said slowly: 'Up to a point, we can clear the thing up.'

'You know about it?' gasped Regina.

'We didn't know about you or your father,' Loftus said quietly. 'We did know that Quayle needed watching, and we've had an eye on him for some time.'

He plunged into a story, circumstantial to some degree but factual in other ways. He evaded any direct statement of the reason for his, and the Department's, interest, creating the impression that it was a branch of Scotland Yard without emphasising it in so many words.

Sir Edmund Quayle, of S.1 Branch of the Ministry of Economic Warfare, had been on the suspect list for some time; Loftus allowed it to be gathered that he was suspected of espionage, but did not say so. Quayle had been watched by a member of his staff actually employed by Department Z. No direct evidence against him had been discovered, but it had become clear that he was a frightened man.

'One of the peculiar things we discovered,' said Loftus, 'was that confidential members of his staff were frequently applying for transfers. Quayle's temper was fiery, and he was always quarrelling. Looking closer into it, we found that the men who wanted a transfer from his Department were those who had been with him six or seven months, and that all newcomers—his staff, of course, was constantly changing—liked him.'

Regina interrupted.

'I remember my father saying that he rather liked the man, just after he started working with him.'

'H'm,' commented Loftus. 'More evidence of the peculiar temperament of Sir Edmund Quayle. Of course, it could be that he grows tired of familiar faces and gets rid of them, fixing it by driving them into asking for a remove.'

Regina hesitated, and then said:

'I was prejudiced against Quayle because I knew he'd worried Father a great deal before the accident, but I didn't go so far as to think he might be a spy.'

'Let's analyse the position as far as it goes. You suspect Quayle or a Mr. X. We suspect Quayle. Your father was a victim of the gentleman's temperament; so were other people whom we have met. One of his assistants recently brought a case for libel and slander against him, but lost it. He dislikes Quayle, too. So the result is, three against Quayle.'

Craigie leaned forward and took a meerschaum pipe from the mantelpiece near him.

The room of Loftus's flat, where they were sitting, was a large one, comfortably furnished. Regina found herself wondering whether Loftus was married. Then she set that question aside as she watched Craigie filling the large bowl of his pipe. Although Loftus went on talking, she eyed Craigie with a new, sharper interest, remembering that she had heard of him before.

She had heard, also, of Department Z.

She experienced a quick flurry of excitement. Loftus and Craigie, of course, were in Department Z. Sometimes the Press published incredible stories of the activities of the Department, often the more popular papers gave lurid hints of the under-cover work operated by it. Hitherto she had not associated Mike and Mark Errol with Department Z, but now she knew what Aunt Bess had meant when she had talked of the Errols being 'something to do with the police'.

'When we've finished the analysis,' Loftus went on quickly, 'we come to the conclusion that Quayle wants plenty of attention. Now I can tell you that the reason he hasn't been removed from his position at the Ministry is because we want to find out his contacts, if any.'

'Was this the job you wanted Mark and me for?' demanded Mike suddenly.

'No,' said Loftus. 'That was a spot of bother in France. Bruce and Wally have taken it on. Bruce was toying with the idea of having a shot at Quayle, but he switched over without any trouble, and as you've found what we might call a personal interest, you're the man for the Quayle job.'

'I suppose I daren't ask whether I can help?' asked Regina.

Craigie lit his pipe, and glanced from her to Mike, saying:

'The boot's on the other foot, Miss Brent. Dare we ask you to help us? Are you prepared to help us in every way you can?'

# CHAPTER 4
## REGINA IS AMAZED

There was only a short pause before Regina answered. 'Yes,' she said. 'Of course.'

'Good, that's settled,' said Craigie. 'We want you to get in touch with a Martin Ainsworth, Miss Brent. Ainsworth,' he went on so quickly that it was obvious that he had anticipated Regina's answer, 'is a man of about your age, perhaps a little older. He has been with the Ministry of Economic Warfare for eighteen months, and with Quayle for five. A violent quarrel with Quayle led to his resignation from the Ministry, but he was persuaded to return. However, he talked too freely and wrote violent letters about Quayle, who answered in kind, hence the libel case, and Quayle's counter-charges, which of course were substantiated. In view of the court's decision, Ainsworth is being asked to resign this time, and I think he's actually left the Ministry today.'

'I see,' said Regina slowly.

'Y'know, I'm getting puzzled about Quayle,' declared Mike. 'What's the sense in it? Everyone suspects him, and he's an obvious trouble-maker. Even if he weren't suspected, why should he be kept on?'

'Because he's good at his job,' said Craigie quietly.

'Oh, well,' said Mike amenably, 'I suppose there's some sense in it. What did Ainsworth do?'

'His job was to co-ordinate reports from occupied countries on the effect of the blockade,' said Craigie. 'That is Quayle's job, also. There are a lot of reports which get into the country unofficially, and they sift the genuine reports from the fakes or the exaggerations. Because of that, Quayle has a great number of contacts with people in occupied Europe, and his opportunities for using the contacts against us, instead of for us, are obvious. Ainsworth went as far as to accuse Quayle of dealing with enemy agents, but that part of the case was heard *in camera.*'

'And what do you want me to do?' asked Regina quietly.

'That's easy,' said Craigie. 'Ainsworth has few friends, and we haven't found it easy to get confidential reports on him. It's possible that he has evidence which he hasn't disclosed, or evidence which he knew would not stand up in court but would be good enough for us to act on. In brief, we want to find out why he made his accusations against Quayle. It could have been spite, but we want to make sure.'

'How shall I meet him?' asked Regina practically.

'That will be arranged,' Craigie assured her.

Little else was said of the project during the next hour, although it remained clear that Mike was troubled. Other things, however, amazed Regina.

In the space of fifteen minutes two Department Z agents received instructions by telephone to visit Lady Beddiloe, at her home near Bath, to make sure that no one broke in; the purpose being to safeguard the papers in James Brent's box. Two others were instructed to come to the flat, and thereafter to follow Regina until further notice. A report was received, also by telephone, from the agent who was watching Martin Ainsworth; the report was brief, for Ainsworth remained in his Chelsea flat—from which, it was said, he had not moved since the verdict had been returned against him. Craigie believed that the £1,000 damages, and costs, with which Ainsworth was faced, were more than the man could afford.

The thoroughness of the Department's arrangements so astonished Regina that she talked of little else while she and Mike walked from Brook Street to the Cumberworth, a large hotel off Piccadilly. Their rooms had been booked, and Regina's luggage already installed. Mike had collected what he needed for a night from his Brook Street flat, and was staying at the hotel simply because he preferred Regina not to be there alone.

Mr. Martin Ainsworth closed a book irritably, and turned over in bed.

From his window the tops of the funnels of a river steamer or a small cargo boat were visible, giving off dark smoke. A tug was hooting on the river, while the clamour of traffic from the Embankment hummed through the room.

Ainsworth glanced at his wrist-watch, which was resting on a small table next to his bed. It was half-past eleven, and he scowled defensively, but did not immediately get up. When he did, he went into a small adjoining room, put on a kettle, brushed his teeth, and then made tea. He sat on the edge of a chair, looking unamiably out of the window on to the swift-moving traffic on road and river.

A nearby clock struck twelve before he finished his tea.

He washed and shaved, peering intently into the mirror. He was always interested in his face. It was dark-skinned and regular, and rather too thin; people said that this angularity made him look distinguished, or even aesthetic. His brows were well-marked, and he had a close-clipped black mous- tache around which he drew the safety razor carefully. His eyes were hazel in colour, and his brows were drawn together in a frown which held a hint of petulance and more than a hint of anxiety.

Dressed, he regarded himself in a wardrobe mirror, and said aloud:

'I *must* do something. It's no use going on like this.'

The truth of the matter, had he cared to admit it, was that there was nothing he could do. He was in a cleft stick, and knew it. There was no one in the world to whom he could appeal for the thirteen hundred pounds required for the costs and damages awarded against him. At a pinch he could get together four hundred. He supposed he would have to make an offer of part payment, or Quayle would carry the case further, and get him sent to prison.

Ainsworth muttered under his breath, picked up a walking-stick and a trilby hat, and stepped to the door. As he opened it, he was surprised to see that the door of the flat opposite him, on the third and top floor of the Chelsea house, was open. The flat had been closed for some months, and he had seen no one there for weeks.

He caught a glimpse of a young woman sufficiently strik- ing for him to look at her again. She saw him, and to his surprise smiled in friendly fashion.

'Good morning,' she said.

'Good morning.' Ainsworth raised his hat. In no mood for casual conversation, he nevertheless felt curious, for it was a fact that there was, practically speaking, no one to whom he could talk. The loneliness which had been desir- able when he had been working hard, often into the early hours, was now a curse.

'Am I to have a new neighbour?' he inquired tentatively. 'For a week or two, yes,' said the woman. 'Do you know Mr. and Mrs. Bonnington?' She mentioned the erstwhile occupants of the flat, and went on: 'They've lent me the flat while I'm in London.'

'Oh,' said Ainsworth. 'That's very nice of them. Er—if there's anything you need, just give me a knock.'

Ainsworth went downstairs thoughtfully. She was a beauty, there was little doubt about that. Since the disastrous end to an early marriage, he was not particularly interested in women, but for that matter he was not interested in people as people; now that he was stranded, with nothing to do, no friends, and no interests outside his books, the situation had altered.

He reached Chenn Street, and strolled towards the Embankment.

Those who knew him well would have declared that he was an impractical man. He lived in a world of figures and literature, and apart from a certain vanity in his appearance, which was impeccable, the things of the world passed him by. Certainly he did not notice that a man was walking on the other side of Chenn Street, and continued to follow him along the Embankment.

He could not avoid seeing another man, in dark grey and wearing a black Homburg hat, who approached him on the Embankment. Ainsworth was staring at the water, seeing small pieces of driftwood floating past, when the man in dark grey stopped and said:

'Have I the pleasure of addressing Mr. Martin Ainsworth?'

Ainsworth stared at him.

'Yes,' he said brusquely.

'Thank you,' said the stranger. He was not a prepossessing individual, for his features were irregular, and the

27

well-cut suit sat ill on him. It could easily be imagined that his face would have been set-off more effectively by a coloured choker. His voice was cultured, however, and his manner faintly self-deprecatory. 'You won't know me, Mr. Ainsworth. My name is Lannigan. I think however, that I might be able to make one or two suggestions which will interest you.'

Ainsworth said: 'Just what are you after?'

'My dear sir, don't misunderstand me! We have a mutual acquaintance, and I think our opinion of the gentleman gives us something in common. I mean Sir Edmund Quayle.'

'Quayle is no friend of mine,' Ainsworth remarked icily. 'I wish you good morning.' He moved on.

Lannigan rested a detaining hand on his arm.

'And no friend of mine, Mr. Ainsworth. May I say that I followed the case which you brought against him with deep interest, and I felt that a grievous miscarriage of justice was permitted.'

'And you're right,' said Ainsworth sharply. 'All the same, I don't see what it has to do with you.'

'I hope that you will,' said Lannigan. He hesitated, and then took a card from his pocket. 'Perhaps you will think about it, sir? I do sympathise with you most deeply, and if you find it inconvenient to meet the damages awarded against you, please believe that I will be very glad to help.'

Ainsworth took the card.

Lannigan raised his hat, then turned and walked quickly away.

As he went, Mike Errol, who had been watching the flat and had followed Ainsworth, faced the need of being in two places at once.

Until shortly before Ainsworth had entered Chenn Street, another agent had been with Mike; he had gone for a ten minutes' break and a cup of coffee at the wrong moment.

With a decision forced on him, Mike followed Lannigan along the Embankment, leaving Ainsworth staring down at the card. On one side it announced that Mr. Alfred Lannigan lived at 51a Queen Street, Bayswater. On the reverse side was pencilled:

*£1,400 is a lot of money.*

After a while, he put the card in his pocket. Then he walked slowly towards Battersea, arguing with himself on his best course of action. He did not intend to have anything to do with Lannigan, he declared firmly, and then wondered what Quayle had done to antagonise the other man.

Not until he reached his front door did he remember the occupant of the erstwhile empty flat.

The woman—girl, he thought, was more apt—was standing in front of his door. She looked round with surprise when he approached, and smiled somewhat apologetically.

'I've just been knocking,' she told him.

'Can I help you?' Ainsworth asked promptly.

'I don't know whether I dare beg a spoonful of tea,' she said. 'I've been to the grocer, but he forgot to put the tea in.' She was smiling, and her eyes were very bright. 'Don't bother, if——'

'Of course I can spare it!' said Ainsworth promptly. 'I won't keep you a moment.'

He opened the door, stood aside for her to enter, and then went into the ante-room which served as a kitchen.

Regina, meanwhile, glanced with interest about a small room lined with books. A door leading to a larger room, also book-lined, was open, and she saw the foot of a bed;

the clothes were rumpled, and the corner of a sheet was touching the carpet. She noted this with satisfaction, before Ainsworth returned; he held a cup, half-filled with tea. 'Thank you so much,' said Regina, and paused. 'While I'm here, I wonder if I can worry you about something else? I want to get a daily woman to come in for an hour in the mornings.'

Ainsworth grimaced.

'I can't help there, I'm afraid. I haven't had one for a fortnight myself.' He hesitated, and Regina thought that he looked very young, vulnerable, and rather helpless. 'Er—my name's Ainsworth, Martin Ainsworth.'

'I'm Regina Grey,' said Regina, lying easily.

Smiling a brief farewell, she stepped to her own flat, and immediately brewed tea; she really needed it, but it had been a good excuse to speak to Ainsworth.

A day and a half had passed since she had met Loftus and Craigie. How Craigie had contrived that she should use the flat opposite Ainsworth she had no idea.

Her tea finished, she telephoned Loftus.

'This is Miss Grey reporting,' said Regina with mock humility. 'I think I am making good progress, sir, and he wants a daily woman. I thought you might like to know that.'

'Not a bad idea,' said Loftus promptly. 'You want one too, I suppose?' He chuckled. 'I'll fix it for one to come along, and you can share her with Mr. Martin A. How is he shaping?'

'I think he's worried. Perhaps I ought to say troubled.'

'You're doing fine, Gina. Talking of doing fine, so is Mark, who is off the danger list. I've just had word from Guildford.'

'Thank heaven for that,' said Regina fervently.

'If you can, get Ainsworth talking about his troubles. Put on your sweetest, most sympathetic air; that ought to do the trick.'

She rang off, smiling. Then she sat up abruptly at a ring at the front door bell.

A woman whom Regina had never seen before stood there, smiling a little expectantly. She was a lovely creature. Her smile appeared set, but as Regina saw her and she saw Regina it faded, and an expression of acute distaste, almost of horror, replaced it.

'Good afternoon,' said Regina.

'You—you——' The caller's voice rose upwards, at a loss for an epithet, and her eyes sparked. 'Where is he? Where is Martin?' A pause, and when there was no reply she went on in a voice pitched on a higher key: '*Where is my husband?*'

# CHAPTER 5
## DOMESTIC INTERLUDE

'I beg your pardon,' said Regina.

The woman's voice remained on the high key.

'You know what I mean! I—I didn't dream he would do such a thing, living with another woman, why, why——'

'It is just possible that you mean Mr. Ainsworth,' said Regina coldly. 'He lives in the opposite flat.'

The woman closed her lips, gulped, and then half-turned. She said in a strangled voice:

'Oh, I'm so sorry, what can you think of me? I didn't know—I thought—I mean they told me he was on the top floor, and——'

She showed no poise, yet to Regina she looked the type who would have it in plenty. Her puzzlement increased, and she felt justified in standing there while the other rang Ainsworth's bell. Then she closed her own door nearly, but not quite.

Ainsworth appeared.

She saw his dark, sharp-featured face, his well-shaped lips parting as he saw the caller. For a moment there was utter silence, and then Ainsworth drew a deep breath and said harshly: 'What are you doing here?'

'Oh, Martin, I had to come! When I knew you were in such trouble, I had to come!'

'You've never troubled to visit me in three years, and I don't see why you should start now.'

'Martin, don't talk like that. And we can't talk here anyway; aren't you going to ask me in?'

'Rita,' he said quietly, 'it isn't the slightest use you coming here to kick up a scene. We agreed to part, on your suggestion. I shall be loyal to the agreement. Now, will you go?'

'Oh, Martin!' exclaimed Rita Ainsworth, and there was a catch in her voice. 'I've only come because you're in trouble, I felt I had to help you.'

'I need no help from you, Rita, please understand that.'

He stepped back. Regina could just see him closing the door, and was astonished when Rita flung herself at him. Ainsworth was carried back as much by surprise as by the rush, and the door banged open. Rita stumbled, and fell heavily. Ainsworth backed away, and Regina closed her door. She felt that she had seen too much of that domestic interlude.

Then she heard Rita's voice, high-pitched and nearly hysterical.

'I won't go away! I know what it is, you're living with that Jezebel next door, do you think I don't know the type!'

Regina thought that she heard a sharp slapping sound, but could not be sure. There was a shriek, and then a thud. Unable to restrain herself, Regina opened the door again and stepped to the passage, but she stopped there abruptly.

Ainsworth was standing in the doorway. The woman was already at the head of the stairs, moving quickly. Ainsworth was looking after her. On his right cheek was a welling streak of blood, and several other scratches, already swollen, showed beside it. If he saw Regina he did not immediately acknowledge her. He stood staring at his wife, who rounded the first landing and went racing down the stairs. Her gasping breathing sounded above her footsteps.

Regina said quickly: 'Please forgive me. I heard myself mentioned, and——'

'I owe you an apology,' said Ainsworth slowly.

'Please! There's no need for explanations,' said Regina quickly. She smiled and approached him. 'Don't you think you ought to have that cut washed?'

'Cut?' said Ainsworth. He put his hand to his cheek, and stared at the blood on his fingers. 'I didn't realise that——'

'Supposing we wash it?' suggested Regina practically.

He let her follow him into his flat, and stood without speaking while she bathed the scratch. It was surprisingly deep, jagged where Rita's nails had torn the flesh. As she worked quickly, she thought again that Rita Ainsworth had behaved very differently from 'type', and her puzzlement increased.

The wild fury in Rita Ainsworth's eyes had not disappeared by the time she reached the street.

She turned left, towards King's Road, walking swiftly. Twice she glanced at the nails of her right hand; they were over-long, and painted a deep red, and now little pieces of blood-covered skin adhered to them. Not until she reached King's Road and hailed a taxi did she pay further attention to them. Then she took a handkerchief from her handbag and wiped them quickly, her face without expression as she did so.

She had directed the driver to Queen Street, Bayswater. The cab stopped outside Number 51a. She paid the driver off and hurried up the four stone steps leading to a narrow-fronted house standing cheek-by-jowl with a hundred others.

She entered the house with a key.

She slammed the door behind her, and as she did so a second door opened and Mr. Alfred Lannigan stood in the passage, staring down at her. She glared ahead as she walked past him. Before she reached the stairs he put out a hand and gripped her arm.

'Aren't you forgetting something, my dear?' There was a sneer in his voice.

She wrenched her arm away.

'I'll come down soon,' she snapped, and ran up the stairs without glancing behind her.

Lannigan shrugged and returned to his room.

It was a long one, between the front lounge and the domestic quarters at the rear of the house. Its one window, tall and narrow, looked into a paved courtyard; heavy net curtains were draped across it, so that no one could see in from the outside without getting close to the window.

The room itself was an office more than a study. Filing cabinets lined one wall, a small desk in a corner held a typewriter and some letter-baskets. A larger desk, set in the middle of the room, held two telephones and a litter of papers, with some heavy account books, one of which was lying open with a pen resting on it. There were no pictures on the walls, but two illustrated calendars made some sort of decoration. Books, mostly of reference, stood untidily on the mantelpiece.

Lannigan bit off the end of a small cigar, sat back in a swivel chair, and waited.

Twenty minutes passed before Rita appeared.

She did not trouble to tap on the door, but pushed it open and entered with set lips and staring, angry eyes. Lannigan took his cigar from his mouth and said gently: 'So it wasn't a success.'

'Success! The brute, I'd like to kill him!'

'Now be careful, my dear, be careful,' said Lannigan. 'Perhaps you didn't approach him properly.'

'Three years ago he would have fallen for it,' she cried with dramatic fury. 'He won't forget me in a hurry now. Every time he looks into a mirror he'll remember today. I scratched him.'

'You *scratched* him?' Lannigan said heavily, and looked relieved. 'I thought, for a moment, you had been very foolish, Rita. Now tell me just what happened.'

When she had finished he asked thoughtfully:

'What was the other woman like? Until two days ago the flat was empty.'

'She wasn't bad-looking,' said Rita disparagingly. 'Dark and getting fat. I tried to play the outraged wife, but it didn't come off.'

'You mustn't let it worry you too much,' said Lannigan. 'We failed that way, but it was only one chance. I may have better fortune. You haven't forgotten that he might call here? Be careful when you know that I have visitors.'

'I'm not a fool.'

'No-o,' said Lannigan, and allowed his doubts to register. 'But you're too impulsive, my sweet. *He* wouldn't like that.'

There was a faint emphasis on the 'he', and the woman stared at him sullenly.

'I do all I can for him, and he owes me a lot.'

'Of course, of course,' said Lannigan. 'He is appreciative of that, my dear, but he likes to feel that he gets a hundred per cent service from us all, remember. Now what are you going to do?'

'I'm going out,' snapped Rita.

She left the house and walked along the street without looking about her. She saw, but did not really notice, Mike Errol standing on the opposite side of the road apparently reading a midday paper.

By then Mike knew that the tenant was Mr. Alfred Lannigan, and that he was a bookmaker.

A very large, untidy-looking man turned into the street. Mike knew that he was the answer to his urgent telephone call for more help, and judged his size as being too noticeable for him to be of much use as a shadow. Nevertheless he stared towards Rita Ainsworth and nodded slightly.

The large man nodded in turn, passed Mike without comment, and went in Rita's wake.

Meanwhile, Lannigan was talking into the telephone to a man he often spoke of as 'he'. The man had a deep, resonant voice, and a bluff, hearty manner, evident even over the telephone. He heard Lannigan's report, and then said heartily:

'You tried, old fellow, you did your best. Perhaps he'll come to see you. Don't forget, get all you can from him.'

'Can I come to see you?'

'Yes, yes, of course,' said the hearty voice with all the goodwill in the world. 'You will be careful, won't you? I am not anxious to be brought into the limelight at this interesting stage!'

'I can handle anyone who follows me,' said Lannigan. 'I'll be with you in half an hour.'

He replaced the receiver, picked up his hat, and hurried into Queen Street. He saw no one, not even Mike Errol, for Mike was standing in a porch where he was hidden from Lannigan, waiting until the man had turned the corner before following.

# CHAPTER 6
# LANNIGAN SUGGESTS

Mike did not think that his quarry knew that he was being followed. He trailed Lannigan to a house in Chelsea, some miles away from Ainsworth's flat; Mike reached the house and began to learn all he could about its owner or tenant, in exactly the same way as he had inquired about Lannigan.

He felt annoyed when he heard that the owner's name was 'Smith'.

Mr. Smith was sitting in a luxurious armchair in a luxurious room in a luxurious house. He was not a large man, but comfortably built, displaying an *embonpoint* which he made no effort to disguise. He smiled often and very widely, showing too many teeth. His sleek black hair, slightly streaked with white, was brushed straight back from his forehead. Surrounded by modern but expensive furniture, with some good water-colours on the beige coloured walls, his feet resting on the thick pile of a plain Indian carpet, his beringed hand holding a glass towards a decanter of whisky and a soda syphon on a small table by his side, he beamed into Lannigan's face:

'Now, my friend, what startling idea has smitten you? What can have entered your mind which you cannot say into a telephone?'

'Sooner or later we've got to look after Ainsworth, and it seems to me that it ought to be sooner. If he gets the wrong ideas, he might cause trouble.'

'I had considered that, Lannigan.'

'How are we going to do it?'

'A way will be found,' said Smith.

'Listen to me,' said Lannigan intently. 'Rita called on Ainsworth, and from all accounts they had a shouting match. When she came back she talked about killing him. There was a woman in the opposite flat who heard, and probably saw, her. She—Rita—scratched and marked Ainsworth's face. She's been separated from him for years, but he can still make her red-mad with jealousy. Supposing, then, that she has a fit of jealousy and kills him? We can fix it. We can fix a suicide for her, too, or let the police have her—it won't make much difference either way. If the police have her, we can help them enough to make them think we're on the level. How does it sound?'

'Not perhaps original, but it's an idea certainly. We shall need to kill Ainsworth without making a mystery about it, and a jealous wife can provide a motive which will satisfy most people, as well as the authorities. We shall need a little more time, while you work on Ainsworth.'

'Give him three days,' said Lannigan. 'That ought to be enough. I'll send Rita out with some of the others this evening, and they can get her tight. I'll fix it that Ainsworth crops up in conversation—I'll tie his name up with someone else. If she's drunk, she'll lead off the way she did to me, and there'll be all the evidence we want that she talked of killing him.'

Smith regarded him fixedly for some seconds, and then threw back his head and laughed.

'My dear Lannigan! Such artistic fervour; you really are invaluable! Proceed with this little drama of yours.'

'Right, I'll fix it.' He paused, and then asked: 'How are the other things going, Mr. Smith?'

'Very well, Lannigan, very well indeed. I have an interview this evening with Sir Edmund. Ah! The great Sir Edmund!' Smith's beam disappeared, his face took on an expression of pretentious authority, and his voice deepened. 'I insist, sir, I insist on a full explanation, here and now!' He broke off, and laughed.

'Quayle to a T,' admitted Lannigan admiringly.

'Not Quayle. Sir Edmund!'

Lannigan left the house soon afterwards, and Mike Errol faithfully followed him back to Bayswater. Mike stayed near the house for some two hours. At five o'clock Rita Ainsworth walked quickly along the street and entered the house. Soon afterwards the large man walked amiably along the road, winking deliberately at Mike as he passed. Mike sauntered after him, and they stopped when they were round the corner, but in a position where they could keep the house under surveillance.

'Well, what happened?' demanded Mike.

'I had a good tea, Mike, a very good tea,' said Martin Best. 'We've a date at the Cherry Club tonight, old boy, what about that?'

Mike eyed him in wonderment.

'I don't know how you do it! But she might give us something interesting, so keep the date.'

Their relief, in the shape of two youthful-looking men, came just before half-past five. Best went off without passing 51a again, while Mike sauntered past the house without glancing up at it. Those who had taken his place did not see any movement at any of the windows and assumed that he had gone unobserved.

Mike hurried to Brook Street and Loftus's flat. When Mike had finished his report, Loftus said: 'So now we have to find more about Lannigan and Smith.'

'Smith my hat!' exclaimed Mike.

'Some people are entitled to the name,' protested Loftus. 'We'll get some photographs tonight, and I'll arrange for some of Lannigan and Smith. Now, about Regina. I've been thinking that it will be wise if you don't go to the Chelsea flat. If Lannigan is interested in Ainsworth, and he is, he might recognise you. She'll have to be looked after, but I don't think you're the man for the job at the moment. Sorry.' He smiled, and Mike scowled but raised no further objection. 'I wish we knew how deep this business was,' Loftus went on. 'I've combed that diary through and found little, except mention of three people who appeared to annoy Regina's father nearly as much as Quayle did. He didn't know them at the office, but saw them sometimes in the evening.'

'Am I seeing them?' asked Mike.

'One of them,' corrected Loftus. 'I've arranged with Regina for you to go through the contents of the box, and the man her father didn't like lives on the outskirts of Radstock. He's a Colonel Thomas Ratcliffe. He owns some shares in a colliery company there, and you can offer him another five thousand, at par. It will look as if you're a stockbroker's tout.'

'Can do,' agreed Mike, a little lugubriously.

'There's a train about half-past seven in the morning. I think I'll have someone else at the Cherry Club to watch Rita Ainsworth,' Loftus continued, 'so you can sleep in peace.'

'Bill, you're putting something across me. Everything was fixed up too smartly when I brought Regina along. What *is* behind it?'

'I don't know, Mike. I didn't know then. All I do know is that we had a note in the records that some papers which Regina's father was preparing before he died were "lost" for three days after his death. We just had that, and no more. When you telephoned the other evening, we looked up Brent's record, and found it. Add that to the fact that we've been interested in Quayle, and his assistants, for some months, and you have as much as any of us know. We can't find what Quayle is doing, and we're not even sure that he's doing anything. But it's a case we must work on, especially since Regina was followed by Lannigan, and Lannigan is interested in Ainsworth's wife. As she's been separated from Ainsworth for a long time, the most likely reason for her visit is one prompted by Lannigan.'

'You're a plausible beggar! Where's Craigie?'

'At Number 10.'

'What's brewing? Anything about this show?'

'No. Hammond and Wally came back from France this afternoon, with some news about one or two of the hot-spots there, and they want a full report at Downing Street. Hammond's with Gordon, telling the tale.' To neither of them did it seem remarkable that two agents had been to Occupied France and back within forty-eight hours, for it was a normal enough thing for Craigie's men. 'The only way it affects us,' added Loftus, 'is that Hammond's back sooner than we expected, and when he's had a good night's sleep he can have a look at the Quayle end.'

Mike nodded, and left the flat to go to his own, only a few doors away.

Loftus was pouring himself out a drink when he heard a key scrape in the lock of the door. With a smile he stood up, and was taking another bottle of beer from the cabinet when Craigie and Hammond entered.

'You're just in time,' he greeted them.

'Good,' said Hammond, but there was a lack of heartiness in his voice which made Loftus look up abruptly.

Hammond was a 'brown' man. He was dressed in brown, his hair and his eyes were brown, his moustache, cut close but covering all of his upper lip, was of the same nut-brown colour. As Loftus's successor as leader of the active list of the Department's agents, he was doing an admirable job.

Loftus unscrewed the stopper, and said quietly:

'Now what's the trouble?'

'What isn't the trouble?' asked Hammond. Larger than Craigie but smaller than Loftus, he walked with a lithe, easy step, and sat leisurely on the corner of the desk. 'I haven't wanted a drink so much in years. Here's how.' He drained his tankard, put it on a newspaper, and thrust both hands deep in his pockets.

Then Craigie said:

'It's just possible that what we've heard is connected with Quayle. If it is, we haven't long to work in, Bill.'

'How long?' asked Loftus quickly.

'A fortnight,' interpolated Hammond slowly. 'A fortnight at the most, and we want six months.'

Craigie said quietly: 'That's not a joke, Bill. Bruce and Wally brought some papers back from France. They were in code, and they were deciphered between the time that we left here and went to Number 10. They prove conclusively that Vichy has been bartering with Berlin, giving details and advance information about our Commando raids on the French coast. They account for the strong opposition we've had recently. Since there's a leakage about the raids, it's possible there's a bigger one, concerning our plans for a general invasion of the Continent. There hasn't been a more serious leakage of information during the war.'

# CHAPTER 7
## AINSWORTH IS CONFIDENTIAL

Loftus did not alter his expression except to draw his brows together in a deeper frown.

'I'm trying to see why we've only a fortnight,' he said. 'If the leakage is working now, news of anything we've planned for fourteen days hence has reached the other side, so it will have to be cancelled.'

Craigie said quietly:

'It's complicated, Bill. Roughly, this is the position. We've a man in Vichy who sees these reports when they get through. A code-message from him dated last night says that no report of any immediate operation has reached French headquarters. It comes from this country, and we might be able to check it.'

Loftus half-closed his eyes.

'Let me get this straight. Vichy is getting hold of super-super confidential dope about our raids. Surely, then, the present invasion plans will have to be altered.'

'Plans are now well advanced,' said Craigie slowly. 'Some of our people are over there at this moment. A big percentage of the underground movement in France is already prepared. True, they can be stopped, but if they are, it means the end of invasion hopes for this year, and another winter might give Germany time to get together again. Does that make it easier to understand?'

'Yes,' said Loftus. 'But I don't see how the "fortnight" comes into it. This information might be on the way to Vichy now.'

'It's not likely,' said Craigie. 'We've been told that the news generally arrives twelve hours, neither more nor less, before the projected attack. The reason for that isn't obscure. There's a release of the plans about fifteen hours before the raids take place—a general release to all commands involved. As soon as they're sent round, someone hocks them to Vichy. As the big attack isn't coming off for fourteen days, the probability is that a similar process will work there.'

'I suppose so,' said Loftus doubtfully. 'When you say invasion in a fortnight, do you really mean it?'

'The official version is a large-scale raid and a prelude to invasion if general conditions are suitable.'

'So we're really getting down to it,' said Loftus slowly. 'Well, well.' He drew deeply on his cigarette, and regarded Hammond with a crooked smile. 'You've unearthed something this time, Bruce! Who's going to look after the Vichy end?'

'I'm sending Tallboys over tonight. He'll contact Stewart, who sent the message, and they'll keep an eye on Vichy and what happens there. If the information gets through they'll be able to send a warning and we can arrange a last-minute cancellation. Hershall agrees that it's the only line to take.'

'I can imagine that the P.M. doesn't like it,' said Loftus reflectively. 'It's a wonder he hasn't stamped over here and started telling us what to do.'

'He said he'd be over,' said Craigie.

Loftus and Hammond looked along Brook Street, and suddenly they stiffened, for a small party of men turned the corner. The leader was a man of medium height, with rounded, packed shoulders and a broad, pale face. Jutting from his lips was a cheroot, which gave him a formidable, aggressive air. He wore a round hat, and carried a walking-stick which he swung vigorously.

Behind him were two well-dressed men whom Loftus knew to be members of the Special Branch at Scotland Yard.

Hammond glanced at the big man, smiling.

'So you were right, and here he is,' he said.

'Ye-es.' Loftus glanced in the other direction. 'There are times when I wish he wouldn't wander about so carelessly as he does. Think what a man with a machine-gun could do!'

'Why think about it?' demanded Hammond.

'Force of habit,' said Loftus shortly.

He continued to look about the street, and Hammond followed his example, while the Rt. Hon. Graham Hershall, Prime Minister of Great Britain, stamped along the pavement, energy, decision and urgency in every movement.

A car turned the corner of the road. Loftus and Hammond peered towards it, but for a moment they said nothing. The car gathered speed, and both men saw a movement at the near-side window. It was no more than a movement of something on which the slanting rays of the evening sun glistened.

Hammond moved fast. His right hand went to his pocket, his left elbow cracked against the window pane. The report of breaking glass echoed high and loud about the street, and Hershall glanced upwards in surprise. Hammond leaned out of the window with an automatic in his right hand, while Loftus bellowed in a voice which carried for half a mile;

'Get down, Hershall! Get down!'

Hershall hesitated for no more than a split second, and then flung himself forward. Behind him, one of the Special

Branch men did the same thing. The other snatched a gun from his pocket.

Hammond fired towards the car.

At the same moment a spray of bullets from a tommy-gun swept the pavement, the staccato tapping loud and clear. The roar of Hammond's gun, as he fired four times, drowned the lesser note. Loftus, unable to move swiftly because of his leg, had to stand and watch.

He saw the policeman who had drawn a gun fall head-long. He saw the little clouds of dust and chippings from road and sidewalk going into the air as a bullet struck not an inch from Hershall's feet. He heard shrieking and shouting from the far end of Brook Street, and saw the car slew to one side, a rear wheel punctured by Hammond's bullet.

By then Loftus also had a gun out.

The car lurched sickeningly, while Hammond climbed through the window, lowered himself, and then dropped to the pavement. As he fell, Loftus saw that the driver of the car was getting control again, and in spite of the flat tyre was going at speed.

*The driver turned the car towards Hershall.*

Hammond steadied himself on the pavement not twenty feet from the car and only five or six from Hershall. He knew that nothing could save the Prime Minister if the car continued on its path, and he ran forward, firing at the driver. His bullets passed through a small gap in the window, and he saw the man sprawl forward; but the car did not change its course.

It did slow down.

The man with the tommy-gun at the back had lost his hold, but regained it then. He trained the gun on Hammond, but before he fired Loftus fired twice. One of

49

the bullets knocked the snout of the machine-gun aside, the other struck the gunman in the shoulder.

Hammond reached the car.

The window was only half down, but he pushed his hand through, and when he exerted pressure the gap widened. He leaned forward and gripped the steering wheel, jammed into position by the weight of the driver, who had fallen against it. Hammond forced it round; the car altered its direction, and the engine stalled.

Half in and half out of the car, Hammond could not see what was happening.

Loftus and Craigie, who was at the front door by then, saw Hershall scramble to his feet while the car still moved towards him, and back away. The Special Branch man, who had also gone down, deliberately jumped in front of Hershall to take the first shock of the crash if the car came on. But Hershall was out of danger a split-second before Hammond turned the wheel.

Craigie stayed in the doorway.

By then a hundred people were in Brook Street, some standing and staring, others running. Police whistles were shrilling out, the heavy stamp of feet was thundering in the air.

Craigie joined Hershall quickly.

'Get me out of here!' snapped Hershall. 'Quick, now!'

He rushed past Craigie into the hall of the house. Craigie stood across the threshold as half a dozen people converged on the door. The Special Branch man was shouting to uni-formed constables who had drawn near. Confusion reigned for five minutes or more, but gradually the crowd dispersed, although whispers that Hershall had been seen were on the wing before long.

Hammond squeezed himself from the car, and policeman and officers surrounded him. The driver was dead; the bullet hole in his temple made that obvious. The passenger, with the tommy-gun still in his hands, was slumped back, his lips parted, his breath coming stertorously. He was wounded in the shoulder and in the chest.

The Special Branch man reached Hammond, and said urgently:

'Shall I look after this, Mr. Hammond?'

'Good man—yes,' said Hammond. He smiled briefly, saw the crowd being hurried along by the uniformed police, brushed his hair back from his forehead, and approached the house where Loftus lived. Craigie remained on the doorstep, unsmiling, his lips drooping.

'How is he?' asked Hammond quickly.

'As well as you and I,' said Craigie.

Hammond drew a deep breath, nodded, and stepped inside. Craigie closed the door, and they hurried up the stairs, quite confident that everything would be looked after outside. As they approached the flat, the door of which was open, they heard Hershall saying:

'Ring No. 10, Loftus, will you? Tell them to make sure that no sensational stories about me get in the Press.'

'Right,' said Loftus.

Hammond and Craigie watched him lifting the telephone. Hershall was standing in the middle of the room with a whisky-and-soda in his hand. The knee of one leg of his trousers was torn, and his coat was dusty, otherwise he looked none the worse for the misadventure. He screwed up his eyes at Hammond, and his mouth curved.

'Thanks, Hammond,' he said.

'Don't thank me,' said Hammond, brushing himself down. 'It was Loftus who thought what a beautiful target you would make if you came.'

Soon afterwards the Special Branch man came up to report that the machine-gunner was seriously injured, and on his way to the nearest hospital. His pockets had been emptied, while all particulars about the car had been obtained. The man wanted to telephone Scotland Yard to get necessary inquiries on foot without loss of time. He did so, finished, and then said to Hershall:

'I'll be downstairs when you want me, sir.'

'H'm,' grunted Hershall. 'Willis, how is Gordon?'

The S.B. man said quietly:

'He was killed outright, sir.'

'Oh,' said Hershall. He rubbed his upper lip slowly, looking at Willis, frowning, with a far-away look in his eyes. 'I'm sorry. Both of you did wonderfully well. You get off, Willis. I'll get these gentlemen to see me back. Go and see Mrs. Gordon personally, extend my deepest sympathies, and—go on, go on,' he added gruffly. 'You know what to say. Find out if there's anything at all that she needs.'

'Very good, sir,' said Willis.

Loftus closed the door behind him.

'You'll know why I'm here, Craigie. Have you told Loftus?'

'Yes.'

'What do you make of it?' Hershall demanded. 'You've usually got something in the way of ideas.'

'Until we've had a little more time we can't say much about it, sir. We might pick up something from the man in the car, or the car itself——'

'No need to assume that the attack and the other trouble are connected,' barked Hershall.

'Equally there's no need to assume they're not,' retorted Loftus. 'But there's a chance that the information leakage is connected with the Quayle business. There are half a dozen subversive organisations at work in the country, as you know, including the one which we call Quayle's because we don't know any more about it than that it might centre about him. The other five are doing work which we can keep track of—I think it's certain that none of them is in a position to get the information which Vichy is dispensing. Consequently we have to assume that the leakage is from the Quayle group, or through a group we know nothing at all about. We've something developing in *l'affaire Quayle*, and within a few days we should have it pretty well closed up—or opened out, take your choice.' He pushed his chair back and stood up, his eyes fixed on Hershall's. The Prime Minister returned his gaze steadily.

'It might be Quayle, yes,' Loftus went on in a taut voice. 'We can find out. When we've done that we need to find who passes the information through to Vichy. I mean the French agent. Have they always received accurate information?'

'Yes,' said Hershall bluntly.

'There's a chance here we haven't had before, sir, a chance in a thousand. Are there any minor raids planned before the big one?'

'Yes,' said Hershall.

'When does the first one start?'

'In forty-eight hours.'

'And the obvious thing to do is to cancel it,' said Loftus, 'to give us time to trace the leakage. Isn't that so?'

'We have just decided to do that,' said Hershall.

'I hope you'll change your mind,' said Loftus slowly. 'It would be better for it to go on, to let the information get through to Vichy. It can be smaller than was planned, the losses need not be heavy. The thing is that if Berlin learns through Vichy of another raid, and it comes off, Berlin is going to rely on that source of information, and, by Gad, we can work from that! If Berlin places full reliance on this source of information, *and we can control that source, passing through whatever information we want them to have,* we can use it to our own advantage, it will be the biggest boomerang ever used. I've been working against Hitler's Intelligence Service for ten years, and I've never yet evolved a way of making him believe he's got genuine information when it's really false. Can you see the possibility, sir? Craigie could find you two hundred men to volunteer. Just a single raid coming off to time, and advice of it circulated through the usual channels. Can we have it?'

'I don't see why not,' said Hershall quietly. 'But before we can do anything on a large scale, Loftus, we'd need much more information than we have at present.'

'Of course,' said Loftus. 'I see that. Tallboys and Stewart are in Vichy. Bruce, you'll have to go over there and work with them. We've got to find who is actually delivering the stuff and be able to give him the wrong goods. Gordon and I can look after the English angle.' He broke off abruptly. 'If only we had more time!'

'Time is all-important,' said Hershall deliberately. 'But I agree with you, Loftus, if we can deceive them in the few days at our disposal it might spell the difference between moderate and complete success *now*. Craigie, you'll come and see me tomorrow afternoon, and let me know how things are going. I came here to tell you people to get a move on, but upon my soul you've given me plenty to do.' He turned to the door. 'Don't forget, by the way, that I don't want anything—*anything*—in the Press about the business outside.'

'Just a minute,' said Loftus sharply.

'Eh?' Hershall was surprised, and turned about.

'If we're going to bluff Berlin, why not do it in earnest?' asked Loftus. 'If they think you're hurt, they'll be cock-a-hoop, especially if the attack on you was managed by the organisation which is selling the information.'

'Are you suggesting that I allow it to be thought that I am seriously hurt?'

'Don't you think it's worth trying?' said Loftus.

# CHAPTER 8
# THE IDEA TAKES SHAPE

The rumour that the Prime Minister was injured spread through London. The speed of it convinced Loftus and the others that several of the enemy's agents had been watching and that a widespread organisation was immediately put into action, to send the story about.

It reached many places, but because Regina 'Grey' had not been out since early afternoon it did not reach her.

Regina had no idea of the ramifications of the affair in which she was involved, but was set on doing all she could to make sure that her part was carried through successfully. Consequently she debated the wisdom of making another approach to Ainsworth that evening. She had the radio tuned in softly, and was busying herself preparing an evening meal when there was a ring at the front door bell.

Ainsworth stood on the threshold when she opened the door.

One of his cheeks was covered with sticking plaster, which made his smile seem stiff and apologetic.

'I—look here, would you mind if I came in for half an hour? You must have heard something of what my wife said this afternoon, and it's only fair to—I mean I'd like to...'

In a little less than an hour Regina had heard of the libel case and Ainsworth's hatred of Quayle, a little of the tragedy of his marriage, and more than a hint of the fact that the damages awarded against him were so substantial that he would have difficulty in avoiding bankruptcy. But she came to the conclusion that those anxieties were minor compared with Ainsworth's regret that he had lost his job. When he stood up at last and prepared to go, she made a casual remark about being glad that she had so pleasant a neighbour.

'I'm afraid I must have bored you terribly,' said Ainsworth awkwardly. 'I really can't understand what made me talk so freely. I—look here, would you care to come out for a drink?'

He stood looking at her a little helplessly, and even had the circumstances been different she doubted whether she would have been able to bring herself to refuse. She arranged to be ready by nine-fifteen, and when he had gone, telephoned Loftus immediately.

'You're doing almost too well,' said Loftus. 'Keep at him, Gina, this might break into something bigger than we expect. Have you heard any rumours?'

'What about?' asked Regina.

'You haven't heard the one I'm thinking of or you wouldn't ask that,' said Loftus. 'Come through again if there's anything unusual, and meanwhile, good drinking! Just a moment.' He broke off, and she heard him speaking to someone else in the room. A deep voice said 'Cherry Club'. Loftus went on: 'Just in case you should fall for a coincidence, don't go to the Cherry Club.'

'Why not?' asked Regina pertinently.

'Because his wife will be there,' said Loftus. 'We're working her end too. Goodnight, my sweet.'

At half-past nine, in a nearby public house, a little man with a bowler hat and a glass of beer in his hand whispered hoarsely to Ainsworth:

'Have you heard, sir? Have you heard? It's about the Prime Minister. Everyone's talking about it, sir. It happened somewhere in the West End this afternoon. Badly hurt, they say he is. Machine-guns.'

'Did you see it?' asked Ainsworth coldly.

'Well, I didn't exactly see it, but——'

'I know, I know,' said Ainsworth, and Regina was amused by his manner and his sharpness. 'A friend of a friend knows someone whose friend saw it. Haven't you learned not to believe rumours yet?'

The rumour also reached the Cherry Club, even earlier. The club's little establishment was in the cellar of a large house in Garton Square, within easy distance of Piccadilly and Oxford Street. Its clientele, as Tannadice, the manager, made clear to everyone, was absolutely exclusive. There was drink and gaiety, the decorations were excellent and in good taste, and the club was well patronised. The cellars in which it was housed were large enough to accommodate two hundred people at a time without discomfort, and if the dance floor was small and therefore grew overcrowded on the evenings when business was good, no one could reasonably complain about that.

Best had been a member of the Cherry Club for some time (as had other members of the Department)—a fact which he had mentioned with some pride to Rita Ainsworth. When he arrived there, a little before the appointed time, the bar was nearly deserted and the orchestra was not playing.

Tannadice was standing near the bar.

'How are you, Mr. Best? It is some time since I have had the pleasure of seeing you.' He was in the middle of extolling the virtues of his chef when Rita Ainsworth entered.

A petulant expression on her pretty face made Best wonder what had happened since he had last seen her.

'Hallo, pet,' he said. 'On time, marvellous creature!' He towered over her and beamed down. 'What'll you have?'

'Give me a gin sling, Percy,' said Rita to the barman. 'What a life this is! Heard the rumour, Tanny? Hershall's dying.'

Tannadice stared. Percy, behind the bar, backed and knocked his shoulder against a row of bottles which were just behind him.

'He was shot-up this afternoon, somewhere near the Haymarket, I think.' She finished her drink and pushed the glass across the bar. 'So what? Fill it up, Percy.'

Best raised an eyebrow.

'So she's going to get tight,' he thought warily. 'I wonder if I want her tight, or whether she'd be better sober?'

She kept sober until after dinner, but mixed her drinks recklessly. The club was filling up by then, and in the next room the orchestra was playing—the dining-room was in an ante-room, the dance floor surrounded by chairs and small tables for casual drinks and snacks only. Best spotted two other Department Z agents, who completely ignored him, and saw several eyes turned towards Rita.

Rita's lips tightened when she saw a small party weaving their way through the tables, two men in uniform and two women. She finished a bottle of inferior champagne, hiccoughed, and turned to Best:

'What about dancing, Mountain?'

Her lips parted, showing her fine white teeth, but she did not look as if she was laughing or happy.

Best wiped the perspiration from his forehead as the dance ended, and she said:

'What about a drink?'

'Surely, surely,' said Best. He allowed himself to be led to a small table near the quartette. Of the malevolence in Rita's expression there was no doubt at all. When the drink came, another gin sling, she sipped it, hiccoughed, and then leaned forward with her elbows on the table and said deliberately:

'Rotter, that's what he is.'

'Oh,' said Best, startled. 'Is he? Who?'

'My husband,' said Rita with the same slow deliberation. 'So are all his friends. Rotters!' She shouted the word, and several people glanced anxiously towards her, Tannadice included. The quartette were not smiling, and the orchestra was having a rest, so that her words travelled clearly.

She stopped abruptly, for one of the men in uniform approached her steadily.

The newcomer was a man of medium height, thin-faced, with peculiarly light eyes. He had two pips, but looked nearer forty than thirty. His mouth was little more than a long thin line, and Best could not find any prepossessing feature about him.

'Good evening,' said Best, very stiffly.

'I object to being called a "rotter".' said the lieutenant harshly. 'And I won't stand for it.'

Rita peered up at him, her eyes glittering.

'That's what you are, and if you don't like the word, I can think of another which might be more suitable for you and all the rest of Martin's gang. You always meant to get him away from me, you always said you'd ruin our marriage! And he believed your lies, the fool, he believed them! Why, if he was here I'd tell him what I think about him. I'd——'

'That's enough!' snapped the lieutenant. 'We've heard enough of your threats before.'

'Threats!' she screamed. 'Threats! One day I'll kill him, I'll make him pay for the way he's treated me! I'll make him suffer, I'll kill him, I'll——'

'You'd better get her out of here,' the lieutenant said coldly, 'and if you've any influence with her at all, make her realise she isn't doing herself any good talking like this.'

'Er—hardly your business,' said Best. But he looked towards Rita, and added gently: 'I say, old girl, d'you think——'

'Have me thrown out, would you!' she shouted, and flung the glass into the man's face.

It broke against his nose and some pieces cut his lip and his cheek. Blood trickled down. There was a scream from someone else, and then two men whom Tannadice had sent came hurrying across the room.

'It's his fault, his fault!' screamed Rita, 'he's turned everyone against me, poisoned everyone's mind! He-'

'Steady, old darling,' said Best. He saw Tannadice's men approaching, guessing their purpose but not proposing to allow them to interfere. He pushed his chair farther back, rounded the table and, without apparent effort, lifted Rita bodily.

She was so startled that at first she did not move or call out, but as he carried her towards the door she started to scream.

# CHAPTER 9
# THE TRIALS OF MR. BEST

Her paroxysm subsided at last, and she began to talk about Ainsworth: she was maudlin, then. How could Martin behave so badly towards her? He had changed, why he had loved her so much that he had married her without a name, cheerfully accepting her illegitimacy. Why should Martin change? She demanded.

Best soothed her. She was listless and lethargic, leaning heavily against him with every step. Her feet dragged, and for some seconds they stood on the pavement outside the club before he helped her into a taxi, and directed the driver to go to the address she gave—51a, Queen Street, Bayswater.

He did not go with her.

Consequently he did not know that Lannigan was waiting on the other side of the door, to lead her up to the two rooms she occupied in the house, and ask her what had happened. She said little, but enough to satisfy him, while the reports Lannigan had received from others who had been at the Cherry Club convinced him that there would be little surprise if she did indeed make an attempt on Ainsworth's life.

Lannigan telephoned 'Mr. Smith', and reported that progress was so far satisfactory.

'Excellent, my dear fellow! Excellent.' Smith's hearty geniality oozed into the telephone. 'First rate idea, there's no doubt about that. Don't take any unnecessary chances, though. Be careful!'

Best also reported the full sequence of events to Bill Loftus, at the flat, and added his belief that in a fit of hysteria or drunkenness, Rita might make an attack on Ainsworth.

'That reminds me, have you heard the rumour that Hershall's been shot? Damn, the business drove it out of my mind!'

'Where did you get it from?' demanded Loftus.

'Rita started it, said he was dying. Seemed pretty sure of herself. Just a rumour, I suppose?'

Loftus looked at him thoughtfully.

'Just a rumour, old son, and I started it.' He smiled obscurely. 'So Rita was very sure of it, was she? She went home after you left her this afternoon and stayed at Queen Street. We had the place watched back and front, and she didn't leave until she left for the Cherry, and she didn't speak to anyone on the way.'

'My oath!' exclaimed Best. 'How did she know?'

# Chapter 10
# Misadventures in Somerset

The two large men eyed one another for some seconds in silence. Loftus relaxed first, stretching out his hand for his beer, and swilling it round thoughtfully.

'Of course, there's a telephone at the house.'

'Telephone?' ejaculated Best. 'I—yes, I suppose.' He looked acutely disappointed. 'Same old Bill. Simple explanation best. I'd worked myself into thinking we'd found something pretty hot at Queen Street.'

His expression suggested that he was something of a fool, and unimaginative to boot, and his manner of talking strengthened that impression; it was quite false, and there were few agents for whom Loftus had more respect.

'So you started the Hershall rumour, did you? What's the great idea, Bill?'

Loftus gave the other man a few more details and saw Best nod with warm approval.

'The rumour spread so fast that it's pretty obvious that hostile agents were watching, or knew about the attack,' continued Loftus, 'and the M.O.I. and the Press are being pretty canny, doing everything but scotching it.'

'Bit of a blow to the great British Public's morale, eh?'

'Yes,' admitted Loftus, 'but it won't be allowed to last too long. It doesn't need to. Just how deep Rita is in the show we don't know yet, but you might get plenty out of her if you handle her properly. Does she know your address?'

'Yes.'

'Good. She might call you if she feels the need for more sympathy,' smiled Loftus. 'Anyhow, get back to the flat and also get a good night's rest, in case she leads you a pretty dance tomorrow. The angle is Rita and Lannigan,' he added quietly, 'and a man named Smith. The thing we want from them is a lead to Sir Edmund Quayle. Do you know him?'

'Know of him,' said Best. 'Knew a fellow who once worked for him. Pretty first-class swine, Quayle. What's he up to?'

'That's just what we want to know,' said Loftus.

An alarm clock burred loudly in Mike Errol's ears, and he started, shot out a hand to switch the thing off, settled down in bed, and then remembered where he was to go that day. He struggled up to a sitting position, rubbed his eyes, grunted, scowled at the clock, and then climbed out of bed, doing none of those things with good grace. But a bath and a shave both refreshed and cheered him.

The Jermyn Street flat, which normally he shared with Mark when they were in London, was a comparatively new one for the Errols; their first flat had been bombed while they had been abroad. The flat, although not unduly so, was small, and Mike disliked it. He disliked even more the fact that Mark was not with him, and while he prepared some toast and boiled an egg, since he knew he could get no food on the train, he brooded on it, and the beginning of this affair for him and for Mark.

Strange that Regina should have come to see them. That, added to what he had since learned from Loftus, introduced a degree of coincidence which worried him.

In a frame of mind which he would have called tetchy, he left the flat and was lucky in getting a taxi to Paddington.

He booked a first-class return to Radstock, the nearest station to Lady Beddiloe's home, and looked about the crowded station. He realised gloomily that there was slim chance of getting a carriage to himself. He was fortunate in being able to buy a paper, and eventually found a corner seat in a carriage where significantly piled army kit showed him that the other three corners were booked.

He watched the people on the platform with jaundiced eye, and as he surveyed them said, half aloud:

'What the deuce *is* the matter with me?'

'I beg your pardon?' said a cheerful voice from the door.

Mike glanced up towards the corridor, startled by the voice and in no mood for cheerfulness from others. He felt a twinge of compunction at the momentary annoyance he experienced at the sight of a short, plump padre, with a round face, pince-nez, and a ready smile.

'Sorry,' mumbled Mike. 'Speaking to myself.'

The rotund gentleman surveyed him placidly for some seconds, made a mild comment about the weather, and then buried himself in his paper.

Mike breathed a sigh of relief, and continued to look out of the window to the platform and the people who were hurrying down the length of the train in an attempt to find a seat. Only five minutes were left before the time of departure. He saw a lieutenant walking more sedately than the others; the man looked into his carriage, then passed on. He had a piece of sticking plaster on his nose. He had grey hair and he looked much older than a junior officer should have been. Mike did not know at that juncture that the officer had been at the Cherry Club the previous evening, and had been instrumental in working Rita Ainsworth up to a pitch of hysteria which had ended in the scene and the chase.

All unaware, therefore, of the need for even greater wariness than he realised, he settled down in his corner. Then the corridor door opened again, this time to admit a porter.

'Mr. Errol 'ere, please?'

'Eh?' asked Mike, startled. 'Oh, yes.'

'Your magazines, sir,' said the porter. 'Your friend just managed to get them.'

He pushed a bundle of magazines into Mike's unwilling hands, and departed, not waiting for a tip.

Mike stared at the magazines and then at the corridor, but there was little time for speculating. Two other officers entered, made no comment, and settled down in their corners. The guard's whistle shrilled out twice, and the train quickened into motion.

'So my friend just managed to get them,' murmured Mike.

Glancing up, he was aware of the bright blue eyes of the padre peering at him over the top of the pince-nez. The man gave a half-smile, and then returned to his *Times*.

There were four magazines. He opened each in turn, half-suspiciously, and in the pages of the last saw a single slip of paper fastened to it with a pin.

Mike widened his eyes as he read:

*I'm around, old boy, but so are some of the other side. Weather eye open! Pat.*

Quite absurdly, Mike glanced up as if expecting to see the leathery features of Patrick Malone, an agent with whom he had never worked on a case, but whom he knew to be on Craigie's staff and who had a good reputation. He did not know that Malone had been in the Cherry Club the previous night.

At Radstock, Mike left the train, and stood for some seconds looking up and down the platform. He saw Malone's tall, rangy figure, a man so typically Irish that usually he was thus identified even before he opened his mouth to betray a fine, rich brogue. He stood idly by the side of the platform as Malone approached, not expecting the Irishman to make any comment.

In front of Malone, separated from him by several civilian passengers, was the thin-lipped lieutenant.

Malone passed without batting an eyelid. Mike raised his eyebrows, let him get well past, and then sauntered towards the station exit. There were several taxis outside, and he was able to hire one just behind the thinlipped officer, who said: 'Do you know where Colonel Ratcliffe lives, driver?'

'Yes, sir,' said the cabby.

'Take me there,' said the officer curtly.

'Mike, my boy,' whispered a voice in his ear, ''tis that man with the mouth like a knife ye want to be wary of. Don't look round, ye fool, I'm after him.'

'Taxi, sir?' asked a man smartly, as Mike watched Malone.

'Oh, yes. Good,' said Mike. 'Beddiloe House, cabby. Do you know it?'

'Of course, sir. Out at Lashley.'

He settled back in the taxi, his eyes half closed, and he did not notice the grey stone buildings or the colliery which seemed to be in the centre of Radstock. Nor did it occur to him then that Radstock, in the midst of the lovely Somerset countryside, was like a north country mining village which had been thoroughly washed and cleaned so that the enshrouding pall of coal and smuts was not apparent.

He recalled enough of the countryside to remember that Lashley, the nearest village to his aunt's house, was between Radstock and Bath, on the Wells side of the road, and was awakened from his reverie when the taxi driver turned left. For the first time he looked about him, and became aware of the brilliant green of the fields and trees, and the cloudless blue of the sky. A perfect day, thought Errol, and wondered how Aunt Bess was keeping.

Then, unexpectedly, the cabby stopped.

Mike leaned forward, mildly surprised.

'What's the trouble?' he inquired amiably.

'It won't take a moment, sir,' said the cabby, opening his door and jumping down. He threw up the bonnet of the taxi, and Mike, vaguely irritated by the delay, heard the rattle of tools. He decided to get out and stretch his legs, and was stepping from the cab when the driver swung round, snapping:

'Stay where you are!'

Mike gaped at him.

He stared at the man's sharp face, then down at the automatic held in a leather-gloved right hand. He was taken so completely by surprise that he obeyed the injuction without hesitation.

The cabby and a gun; no, it was preposterous.

'Get back inside,' the man said next.

There was an indescribably evil expression on a face which had suddenly become ugly. The expression, more than anything the man said, made Mike force himself to be more realistic—and the realism indicated by the situation was for him to obey and get back into the taxi.

'Get in!' the man snapped, and his voice took on a higher note, one which struck Mike as odd and made him eye the man narrowly. Then he saw that there was, after all, the faintest of quivers in the gun hand, and that the man's lips were drawn tightly together and were trembling a little. *The gunman was afraid.*

Mike sank into the rear of the taxi without grace, and turning his coat so that this right pocket was free but just out of the gunman's sight—his own automatic was in it—he felt the cold steel and experienced a sharp sense of satisfaction. He did not need to ask questions to know that the taxi driver had instructions to stop here, and that others were expected soon.

He had climbed from the taxi and forced the issue more quickly than the man had anticipated, thus also forcing a crisis.

He did not shoot, although he could have done so through the window.

He wanted to see those others who were coming, and if he were in sole possession of the taxi they might not show up. He kept his hand about his gun and felt greatly comforted. The driver peered at him through the open door, glancing right and left once or twice as if afraid that someone he did not want would come. Suddenly and without warning they heard the ting! of a cycle bell. Both glanced involuntarily towards the right, where a girl cyclist was turning from the main road and gliding down a slight incline at a good speed.

'Keep your mouth shut or I'll shoot!' the cabby hissed.

The girl sailed nearer, and then passed by, glancing curiously at the taxi. Suddenly she applied her brakes, and before the cycle had stopped, called:

'Can I help you?'

'No, I——' began the driver.

Errol beamed at the girl as she stood astride her cycle and looked over her shoulder.

'That's very nice of you, but someone is bringing us a spare part.'

'Oh, that's all right, then,' said the girl.

'Are you going into Lashley?' asked Mike, very sweetly.

He heard the intake of the driver's breath, but knew that the man would not want to do anything to upset whatever plans he—and others—had in mind.

'Why, yes.'

'You might tell someone at Lady Beddiloe's house that I'll be along in about half an hour,' continued Mike in honeyed tones and without looking at the taxi driver. 'My name's Errol.'

'Oh, yes, sir,' said the girl. 'I work there, I'll tell her ladyship at once.'

'Thanks very much,' smiled Errol.

The girl cycled on, and Errol looked into the vicious face of the driver, whose hand was trembling noticeably and upon whose forehead there was a beading of perspiration. It was novel to be held up by a man so obviously frightened, although there was the risk that if he tried the other too far, jumpy nerves would make him shoot.

'Why, you——' the man began thickly.

'Now, come,' said Errol. 'I can't keep my aunt waiting without sending a message, can I? And if I'm not there in half an hour,' he added dreamily, 'there will surely be inquiries.'

He hoped to sting the man into giving away some information, but failed completely.

He looked through the rear window.

The car which came into sight was an M.G. Sports, a little car with chromium glistening in the sun, and the metal of half a dozen club badges on the radiator and the bumper. It was driven by a hatless man in flannels, and had there been no passenger Mike would have taken it for granted that it was another casual passer-by. But there was a man in the back, a man dressed in drab grey, one whose face Mike was never likely to forget.

It was the man who had shot Mark.

The M.G. snorted and then came to a standstill a few yards behind the taxi. The driver did not get out, but the man in grey hurried to the road and approached the taxi driver.

'Any trouble, Blaney?'

'The swine told a girl he'd be at the house soon,' muttered the taxi driver. 'He's too damned fresh, and——'

The man in grey ranged himself alongside the driver. He had both hands in sight and empty, obviously relying on the cabby for armed support. His thin, lantern face was expressionless as he said:

'He'll learn. Get out, Errol.'

'What, again?' asked Errol, as if injured. 'I've been out once and he sent me back.' He half-rose from his seat and the taxi driver's gun was thrust forward warningly. 'Misadventure in Somerset, we call this, don't we? Sorry about it, but you have rather laid yourself open.'

He fired twice from his pocket.

His first bullet struck the wrist of Blaney's gun hand, and sent the gun flying; the second took the man in grey through the thigh, making him stagger backwards with his arms whirling in an attempt to save himself.

There was a brief moment of startled silence, and then the engine of the M.G. throbbed into violent life.

Mike kept low, with the gun in his hand.

He expected to hear the car change gear to reverse, but the driver came on towards the taxi. Mike saw nothing until its nose reached the open rear door. The gunman was backing desperately towards the hedge, and the man in grey was sprawling out on the road, quite helpless.

*The M.G. went over him.*

The hatless driver was looking straight ahead, tight-lipped. His was a youthful, handsome profile, the fair hair blowing in the breeze created by the speed at which he travelled. There was an ugly, sickening crunch as he passed over the man in grey, and then he cleared the taxi and started to increase his speed along the road towards the nearest corner.

Mike spent no time in horrified exclamation. He swung himself sideways so that he could fire along the road, emptying his gun towards the rear of the M.G. He heard the whang of bullets striking the wings and body, and then the car screeched round a corner.

Mike jumped to the ground.

As he reached the road he swooped down, picking up Blaney's automatic, and with it ran forward at speed. He reached the corner in time to see the M.G. perhaps sixty yards away, scorching towards another turn. He fired twice, but had little hope of doing enough damage to stop the car when he heard the loud report of a tyre-burst and saw the M.G. swerving violently to one side.

'That's got you,' muttered Mike with satisfaction.

He continued to run, filled with a savage anger at the realisation of the cold ruthlessness with which the man had run down his confederate. He thought of nothing else as he neared the M.G., the nose of which was now buried in the bank. The driver, apparently unhurt, was standing beside it. He glanced behind him, saw Mike, and put his hand to his pocket.

Mike missed him with another shot.

A bullet whirred past his head in turn as the hatless man fired at him and then made a standing jump over the hedge. Mike saw him disappear, hands flung upwards to keep his balance, and looked at the hedge to find the lowest part for a jump from the road. It would take some doing, for the driver had been two feet from the ground. Tight-lipped, Mike judged his distance.

As he sailed over the hedge he saw the killer running over a field of stubble.

Mike stood quite still and fired.

The bullet struck the man, who pitched forward in the middle of a stride, tried to save himself by pushing his hand to the ground, failed, and then collapsed. Mike began to run. The hatless man was not unconscious, for he turned on the ground and Mike saw the glint of the sun on his automatic.

'Here it comes,' Mike muttered *sotto voce*, and flung himself down. He heard the whine of the bullet over his head, but he was not hurt, although the other now held the advantage. Winded, his face rasped on the harsh stubble, Mike lost his grip on his gun. He held his breath as a bullet pecked the ground close to him.

He saw the other move his gun a fraction, and then fire again. He rolled over, but there was no need to worry, for the gun fell to one side uselessly, not even a faint click reached Mike's ears. It was hard to believe at first, but he peered towards the other and saw him stretched out, his hands inert. The man's eyes were open, but it was clear that his gun was empty, and that the final effort had taken a great deal out of him.

Warily, Mike drew nearer.

Soon he saw that his bullet had struck the other in the chest. A gingerish sports jacket and a pale blue shirt were both stained with blood, and the stain on the shirt was getting larger. Mike was near enough then to hear the other's heavy breathing, and to see the pain which filled wide-set grey eyes.

Mike stopped and looked down at the man, then went on one knee.

'Not your day,' he said. He lifted the empty gun, tossed it aside, and then pulled open the blue shirt.

Between tight lips the man said: 'Let me alone.'

'No, I've only just started,' said Errol harshly. Memory of the way the fellow had driven over the man in grey was vivid in his mind, no pain nor punishment which the hatless one endured would be too great or undeserved.

The wound was above the heart, but he judged that his bullet had pierced the lung. It would be impossible to do anything but stem the bleeding and then leave the man there while he sent for an ambulance. The other was too weak to make further protest, and stayed quite still while Mike padded a handkerchief over the wound, then looked about for something with which he could bind it.

While he was taking off his tie and the man's belt, he heard a scream from the road, so sudden and abrupt that it made him start violently. It came again, shrill-pitched and strident, high above the laborious breathing of the man on the ground.

# CHAPTER 11
# HOLLOW VICTORY

As far as Mike could see the man he had shot was unconscious; his eyes were closed and his face set and strained. With the screams echoing in his ears he temporarily fastened the wad, then turned and ran across the golden stubble.

He did not try to leap the hedge this time, but searched for a low part and scrambled over.

He jumped down into the road.

It had been a false alarm: a woman was running towards the main Bath road as fast as her short, bandy legs could carry her. A basket was lying by the hedge near the body of the grey man, and groceries and provisions were strewn about, a tin of peas resting in a pool of blood.

The taxi driver had gone, but the cab remained.

He lost no time in getting into the cab, and starting up, heading towards Lashley. It nestled in a hollow fringed by thickly growing beech trees. The grey stone of the cottages and the buildings was mellowed by time and trailing creepers, some turned a glorious hue which he could not fail to notice despite the stress of circumstances.

Mike slowed down as he neared a small garage, a stone building with petrol pumps discreetly placed, doing all it could not to advertise its calling. Motionless beneath a long-nosed car lay a pair of legs in overalls.

Mike spoke quickly: 'I say, can I use your telephone?'

He wanted to shout to the owner of the legs that not three miles away a man lay dead near another grievously wounded, but he controlled the temptation as the other, clambering to his feet with a considerable effort, answered him.

'Aye, welcome, ye'll find un in the office.'

The operator put Mike through without delay to the Bath police. A crisp, clear voice responded after he had asked for the Superintendent on duty.

'Chief Inspector Webber speaking. Can I help you?'

'Yes,' said Mike. 'Inspector, I haven't much time and what I've got to tell you will be something of a shock, so get a pencil handy—good man.' He drew a deep breath, and then went on: 'A man has been killed, another badly wounded, near the Radstock–Bath road, on the by-road to Lashley. There has been gun-play, and one of the gun-men escaped on foot. He is short, rather small, and dressed in a shiny navy blue suit with a peaked cap. He picked me up at Radstock Station,' continued Mike, thinking kindly things of the businesslike inspector. 'He had a taxi, an Austin in good condition.' He peered through the window of the office, saw the number of the cab, and read it out. Then: 'There is an M.G. sports car in the hedge on the same road, and it'll need a breakdown van before it's shifted. That's all, I think, except that my name is Errol——'

'Errol?' asked Webber sharply.

'That's right.'

'A relative of Lady Beddiloe's?'

'Also right,' said Mike. 'And listen, Inspector, this job is urgent. You'll probably get a chit through from the Yard about it, but meanwhile will you look for that cabby—oh, I've just remembered his name. Blaney. And,' went on Mike hurriedly, 'one of the main things is that there's another man wounded in a field near the M.G. He'll need medical attention and an ambulance.'

He rang off and drove back to the scene of the attack.

Chief Inspector Webber was a man of medium height, well built, well knit, pleasant looking, with cool, appraising grey eyes. He had five men with him, including one with a pronounced limp, who hurried towards the body lying in the stubble.

The doctor, thought Mike, after introducing himself.

Webber said: 'We shouldn't be long getting Blaney, Mr. Errol. He's well known in Radstock and around.'

The doctor, was returning, less hurriedly. He reached them as an ambulance arrived from the other direction.

'How is he?' asked Mike.

The doctor, a sharp-faced young man with dark brows, shook his head abruptly.

'Quite dead.'

'Dead!' exclaimed Mike. 'Why, that wound——'

'Didn't die from wounds,' said the doctor briefly. 'He took something. Poisoned himself. What's happening here, Webber, another massacre?'

Mike leaned heavily against the wing of the taxi.

The man in grey was dead, and there was not much left by which to identify him. He had realised when he had first left to telephone the police that the most likely source of information of consequence was the bare-headed man, and he had taken it for granted that the other would be alive, and a fit subject for questioning once the bullet was out of his chest.

Webber continued to eye him curiously, and said without words but with a plain enough gesture that he thought Mr Errol should give him a little more information.

Mike took his wallet from his pocket and extracted a card signed by the Chief Constable of Scotland Yard and counter-signed by the Assistant Commissioner: it authorised Michael Errol to call on the help of the police in any district where he found himself, and stated that Mike was on special business.

'Are there any more victims?' demanded the youthful doctor sardonically.

'Not yet,' said Mike. 'You might be busy during the next forty-eight hours, though.'

Beddiloe House loomed large as Mike pulled up, climbed out, and entered the wide, cool hall. It was a delightful entrance, which never ceased to soothe him, with its polished floor, skin rugs, large open fireplace, and oil paintings covering the high walls. The paintings were mostly of landscapes, although there were two portraits on either side of a doorway leading to the left.

Voices were coming from it.

'Well, I don't know, my boy,' said a pleasant, rather lilting, voice, that of an oldish woman. 'I really don't know what to advise. Of course, Teddy was always different from you, and if he really *believes* in this objecting, well, there isn't much we can do about it.'

'Confound it!' exclaimed a man, a young man, thought Mike. 'He can't keep it up, it's a disgrace to the whole family. A ruddy conchie, my own brother!'

'Do you know, Brian,' said the woman gently, 'I think you're upsetting yourself unnecessarily. It's a matter of conscience—his conscience, not yours. So try not to worry about it. Teddy always went his own way, and I'm afraid we can't stop him. How long are you home for?'

'A week,' said Brian gloomily. 'Well, I won't keep you now, Lady Beddiloe. I—er—I knew you'd understand if I did come. I thought you might have some influence with Ted. May I come and see you again?'

'As often as you like, of course.' There was the scrape of a chair, and then footsteps. A shadow darkened the hall, but the man inside stopped on the threshold and spoke again.

'I still can't understand it, you know. Teddy *has* changed, he's secretive about everything, and he hasn't written to me more than twice in the past six months.'

'I expect he's been busy.'

'Busy! I'd think a lot of myself if I couldn't find time to drop a line regularly to my twin brother!'

Aunt Bess spoke quietly and soothingly, and then the door opened more widely and a tall, good-looking man stepped through.

Mike stepped back a pace and gaped at him.

The newcomer stared in surprise. Mike made a noise in the back of his throat, and the other said:

'I say, are you all right? You look as if you've seen a ghost.'

'Er——' started Mike, and then swallowed hard, with difficulty keeping himself from blurting out that he did indeed feel that he was looking at a ghost: for this youth was the image of the driver of the M.G. who had first killed another, and then, himself.

# CHAPTER 12
## NOT EASY FOR TWINS

Mike continued to stare, so taken back that he could think of nothing to say that would be cruel or ludicrous. He moved only when Lady Beddiloe appeared in the doorway, apparently attracted by the voices. A short, slim, woman, she looked at him mildly before she exclaimed:

'Michael!'

'Hallo, Aunt Bess,' said Mike, and turned to allow himself to be embraced.

If the old lady realised that there was anything strange in Mike's manner she made no comment on it, quietly introducing the two men.

'Mr Michael Errol, Brian Howe.' She smiled at them both. 'I'm so glad you two have met. I've always hoped that you would one day. Brian is the son of a very old friend of mine, Michael, and——'

She went on for a few seconds, while Mike recovered himself and had the inspiration of arranging to meet Howe later in the day for a drink. He imagined that the young naval officer's expression was clearer when he left the house and walked smartly down the drive.

Mike followed his aunt into a tall, airy room of quiet greens and yellows, Louis Quinze furniture, and gilded chandeliers. A handsome room, full of grace and friendliness, like Lady Beddiloe herself.

She wanted to know whether he was all right, and how was Mark? Had Regina visited them, and could they help her? She, Aunt Bess, was inclined to think that there was something strange in what had happened, but she had not encouraged Regina to think so, in case it frightened the child. Not that anything would easily frighten Regina.

He told her the story quietly. He made it clear that the man who had poisoned himself had been a spy: of that there was no reasonable doubt, and he did not raise any. He did not give any details of what had happened on the road, but made it obvious that if Brian Howe learned the whole truth he would feel much worse than if he had just believed his brother to be a pacifist with strong views.

When he had finished, she said:

'Teddy Howe and his brother were never alike in anything but appearance. Teddy was worried all through his life, restless, anxious, uncertain of himself. He was brought up in a wealthy household, and then the family lost its money. It wasn't easy for him, Mike. Brian was always the more placid; nothing really worried Brian. I liked them both, but I was afraid that Teddy would one day do something so foolish that it couldn't be forgiven. And now, if you're right, he has.'

'He has indeed. Nor can I work up even sympathy for him. You wouldn't, if you'd seen what I saw. But that's by the way, Aunt Bess. Where did he live?'

'At Lashley Cottage.'

'That's not far from here,' mused Mike, the shock of his experience wearing off as his mind worked more clearly. 'He'd have all the opportunity in the world for getting a look in that box, wouldn't he? The cabby, Blaney, might have worked with him, of course. Who else lives at the cottage?'

84

'No one all the time,' he was assured. 'Brian goes there when he's on leave, of course, but they're the only members of the family left. There's a daily woman and an odd-job man, but neither of them lives at the cottage. Why, Mike?'

'I'd like to look round there,' said Mike thoughtfully.

After lunch his aunt went to rest, but first showed him Regina's room and the storeroom where the box was kept. She gave him the keys of the box, and Mike spent an hour looking through the relics of James Brent's life, finding papers and sentimental souvenirs, photographs, birth certificates—those and a dozen other things which must have given Regina a lot of pain to look through. He found nothing which might connect with Quayle, or the uncertainties Brent had experienced, and doubted whether there was anything there. Possibly the thieves had wanted the diary, and nothing else. He examined the box for a false bottom or a secret cavity, but finding nothing to indicate either, relocked it and went downstairs.

A few minutes afterwards Webber arrived. He was as quiet and capable as ever, and announced immediately that he had telephoned Scotland Yard and confirmed Mike's bona fides. He wanted to know whether there was anything he could do to help.

'Have you found Blaney?' asked Mike.

'No,' said Webber, 'but he can't have got far.'

'I hope not,' said Mike. 'I don't like some of the things that are happening in this show, especially down here. You recognised the dead man, of course?'

'Edward Howe, yes.'

'Were you surprised?'

'Howe hasn't been popular in the district,' he said. 'I mean amongst the police, I think he was well enough liked by the villagers in spite of his beliefs. The family has been nearby some hundreds of years, and both boys were accepted unquestionably. But his pacifist views have been pretty strongly expressed in some quarters, and he's given us a little trouble.'

'He didn't make his views known too freely locally, surely?'

'No, further afield,' admitted Webber.

'I'm going to have a look through the cottage, Inspector, and it might be an idea if you could put a couple of men somewhere near at hand for me, in case of emergency. I'm going to take his brother into my confidence,' he added. 'You've no objection?'

'Brian Howe's all right,' said Webber with assurance.

'Did Edward have any close friends?'

'I wouldn't say that, no. He had a part interest in one of the old collieries near here. His family owned a seam where there was a disaster some ten years ago, and it was closed up soon afterwards. The company failed, and he was on his beam ends. He had acquaintances amongst the other colliery owners here.'

'Business acquaintances, not friends,' suggested Mike briefly. 'Who would you name as the most familiar ones, Inspector?'

'Mr. Gregory Hanton, of Heath Place,' said Webber, 'and Colonel Ratcliffe, at——'

'I know Ratcliffe's address,' said Mike. 'No one else?'

'I don't think you could name anyone else,' said Webber slowly. 'Of course, they haven't had a great deal to do in common recently, although I've heard rumours that Howe was trying to sell his mine. There may be a few seams left there that could be worked. The only likely man to buy is Colonel Ratcliffe, so they've seen one another several times recently.'

'Ratcliffe's all right, I suppose?'

'Perfectly all right,' Webber assured him emphatically. 'You needn't worry about the Colonel.'

Mike watched the Inspector go with mixed feelings. He felt an empty depression within him, as if he were falling down on his job; another thing on his mind was the task of telling the truth to Brian Howe.

He telephoned Lashley Cottage.

After a long pause, Brian said harshly:

'You're sure of your facts, I suppose?'

'You know the relevant ones,' Mike told him. 'You have to take my word that I'm down here on counter-espionage work, but you can get it checked with little trouble.'

'Oh, I'm not doubting that,' said Howe. He stood up and paced the room restlessly. 'There's been something odd. I've sensed it for a long time. He did his damnedest to prevent me from coming home this time. Tried all manner of excuses. When I got here he tried to be pleasant, but it was a bad effort.' Brian shrugged. 'It all fits in now. It's hard to take, Errol.'

'I want to look through the house,' said Mike quietly. 'Particularly his rooms.'

'We'd better get cracking,' Brian said abruptly. 'Come on.'

They spent two hours in a study on the first floor and a bedroom opposite it. The furniture was old, but the rooms were kept much better than the garden. The search was not arduous, although it was disappointing, for they found nothing. They did discover a metal filing cabinet in the study, with the bottom section locked, but when they opened it, Mike using a screwdriver to force it, the drawer was empty.

'Well, we'd better get downstairs,' said Brian in an abrupt voice, one which held a hardness doubtless induced by the shock he had received. As they reached the hall he turned on his heel and said quickly:

'There's one spot where we haven't looked. The summer-house—an old place in the garden. He did a lot of writing there. Tosh about pacifism!' Brian shrugged, leading the way along the gravel path through a shrubbery and an orchard, where the fruit was hanging ripely on the boughs, beyond which stood the summer-house.

The view was superb, the land dropping away to a deep, fertile plain, dotted with trees. The clearness of the day and the blueness of the sky which formed the distant background made the scene one of incomparable beauty.

Closer to them was a line of tall and stately beeches, their leaves rustling a little in the slight breeze. A long way off, in sight only when they reached the summer-house itself, was Heath Place, the big new house which Mr. Gregory Hanton had built.

'Some view,' said Brian briefly. 'Often spent hours here. See that cricket pitch?' He pointed towards a green patch in the midst of the cultivated land, near Hanton's house. There was a small pavilion there, and a fence ran about the ground itself. 'Often played on it, wonderful pitch. I——'

He broke off abruptly, and turned to the summer-house.

Built of rough wood-facings from felled timber off the estate, it was decaying in places and badly needed a coat of oil or creosote. A large building for its purpose, it was raised from the ground by supports of Bath stone. The door was locked, but there was a key on the ring which Brian brought out.

The interior of the summer-house was dark after the brilliant sunlight outside, and Mike narrowed his eyes as he stepped within. Brian joined him. There were a tiled table and several garden chairs, but nothing else; the place was empty.

Mike took a step towards the door, and then the floor opened beneath his feet and he fell through the yawning cavity.

One moment he was standing and looking at Brian, seeing the taut expression on the man's face; the next he was dropping down what seemed to be a bottomless pit. His stomach heaved, all sense of disappointment disappeared in a surge of overwhelming, instinctive fear. He did not even know whether Brian was coming after him, did not think about the other man, only just recovered himself in time to bend his knees to take the inevitable jolt as he hit the bottom.

He fell into water and then mud.

As he plunged downward, he took in a deep gulp, coughing and retching as the noisome water went into his mouth, dank and evil-smelling. Then he broke the surface, and as he did so something struck him heavily on the shoulder and pushed him under again.

His head reeled, and for a moment he thought that he was going to lose consciousness. Recovering, he straightened up dazedly, over waist-deep in the water.

It was surging violently to and fro from the impact of the fall. He could see nothing; there was only a Stygian darkness about him. But he heard a floundering movement, then realised that Brian Howe's body had followed his own, and struck him as it fell. He groped about beneath the water, and touched something which moved. Drawing a deep breath, he tightened his hold, and found that he was grasping Brian's wrist. In a few seconds he altered his grip and took the other's waist, then pulled him upwards.

He knew then that the man had been doubled up beneath the water, probably unconscious from the fall.

He stood upright, gasping for breath, supporting the sagging body. High above him there was a tiny circle of light, the entrance to the hole. Beyond that he could see nothing, and the water in which he was standing might well have been the Styx itself. He began to feel cold striking at him, and suddenly shivered. He knew that he dared not move until Brian had regained consciousness, if he ever did. Clumsily he felt for his pulse, and discovered that it was beating.

Howe stirred.

He grunted, moved his arms, and then went still again. After what seemed a long time his voice broke the silence, harsh and croaking.

'You there—Errol?' He paused. 'Didn't know—the workings—extended as far as this.'

'What workings?' Mike asked sharply.

'Mines, of course. Knew they were about.' Brian's breathing grew more laborious, but Mike's heart leapt with the realisation that he had fallen down a shaft leading to the old coal mine which the Howes had owned.

'It's time we started exploring a bit, isn't it?' he said.

It took them some time groping through water about the wall, their feet embedded in mud, to find the gap which both knew must exist. Once they found it they began to move along the passage to which it led. At first they had no idea of the width of the passage, but by standing side by side and stretching out their arms they found that by keeping at full span they could touch the wall.

They went on slowly, and after a while found themselves walking on a dry floor. But the darkness remained; their footsteps made echoing sounds which worried them, and they could hear the squealing and scuffling of rats. They did not know how long they had been underground; although they had matches the water had made them useless, and their watches were invisible.

They went on and on, turning corners, stumbling, speaking rarely; and with every passing minute their hopes grew fainter.

# CHAPTER 13
# A SEARCH BEGINS

The fact that both Mike Errol and Brian Howe were missing was suspected by seven o'clock that evening, and presumed by nine. Lady Beddiloe called the police at half-past seven.

By ten o'clock Loftus heard of the disappearance.

He was in Craigie's office at Whitehall, thinking far less about Mike than about news which Craigie had brought from Hershall that evening. Hershall had convinced his colleagues that the rumour need not be scotched for a few days, and by then it was all over the country. It had been spread with such lightning speed that Loftus and Craigie were worried: the agents who had carried the news from London must have been numerous, the recipients of the news equally so. For the first time both men were forced to face the possibility that there was a wide-spread subversive organisation of which they had known nothing.

'Too little is happening,' Loftus said, sitting in an easy chair at the fireplace end of Craigie's office, and looking across at his chief, who was smoking his meerschaum with a deceptive air of peace and satisfaction. 'Gina hasn't got any more out of Ainsworth, except one rather odd comment. He told Regina that it would be a blow if anything happened to Hershall, especially "just now". That "just now" worries me, Gordon. I wonder if it would be wise to put our cards on the table with Ainsworth?'

'I should give Regina another day or two,' advised Craigie.

'You're probably right.' Loftus took a large-bowled pipe from his pocket and began to fill it. 'What about this small raid on the French coast?'

'It's coming off tomorrow night,' Craigie assured him.

'Good. We'll need to tell Bruce.'

By then he had heard from Bruce Hammond of his safe arrival in Vichy: the channels of information and messages to and from France were many, and all of them were reliable. For Loftus and the Department communication with the occupied countries was nearly as straight-forward as that with the neutrals, and in some cases easier.

Consequently before the night was out Bruce Hammond and the agents whom he had met in Vichy knew for certain that the raid was planned for the following night, and also knew where it would be.

A short, dapper man with waxed moustaches, Tallboys left for the coast to find whether any special preparations were made beforehand against the attack. Stewart, a Scotsman who looked in some miraculous way like the most typical of French peasants dressed in new clothes and obviously flourishing—and therefore presumably in Nazi pay—stayed with Bruce Hammond in Vichy.

Like Loftus and Craigie in London, and Tallboys near Boulogne, where the raid was to take place, they felt on edge and impatient for zero hour...

The telephone rang.

It was Superintendent Miller of Scotland Yard, the liaison officer between the Yard and Department Z. Miller had heard from the Bath police of Mike Errol's disappearance, and thought that Craigie ought to know at once.

'Yes, I'm glad you rang,' said Craigie quietly. 'Is there anything else?'

'Nothing you don't already know about,' said Miller, and rang off after a brief exchange of opinions.

Loftus looked at Craigie with one eyebrow raised half an inch higher than the other, and asked quietly:

'For me?'

'Yes,' said Craigie, and explained what had happened.

'Now I wonder what that means? D'you think Mike has seen a trail and started off on it?'

'Without sending a word to anyone?' Craigie looked doubtful.

Loftus said, 'So you take the dark view?'

'Don't you?' countered Craigie.

'I wish to God I could get down there! Pat Malone is busy with the cove who's gone to see Ratcliffe, Martin Best's busy on Rita—most of the fellows are busy, if it comes to that.'

'Wally's free,' said Craigie thoughtfully. 'And Graham is all right, although he'll be tired.' He returned to the desk and lifted the telephone, then gave orders to one Wally Davidson, and an agent who was known to the others as 'Young Graham'. They had instructions to go by road to Lashley that night, and were told that above all things Department Z wanted Mike Errol and Brian Howe found. They received their orders with evident satisfaction, and Craigie was smiling a little when he replaced the receiver.

'Nothing will ever put Wally off, will it?'

'I hope not,' said Loftus fervently.

❧ ❧ ❧

Craigie had little news of consequence when later on he came to the flat. His reports had come in from various quarters, including a telephone call from Best to say that Rita had stayed at the Queen Street house all day. Agents watching both Smith and Lannigan had nothing to report, and there had been no visitors to either house.

A point of interest was that Sir Edmund Quayle had been confined to his home all day, officially indisposed. Agents of the Department and of other sections of British Intelligence were by then working at Quayle's office, but the reports which came through contained nothing to confirm that it was the source of the leakage.

'You know, Gordon, we may be chasing a hare. Quayle isn't in a position to know about the raids.'

'Not necessarily,' returned Craigie, 'but he co-ordinates the information needed for the troops when they land, and prepares a plan of the vicinity for the Admiralty as well as the War Office. Quayle started off by being in the Economic Warfare Ministry, but all his men know the Continent so well that they're really a special Department which works between the Ministry and the fighting services. Quayle and some of the staff in his office prepare the first maps for any area about to be attacked, and therefore know at once what area is under consideration. From there they don't have to go far to get the date and time of the actual assault. They don't even need to know as much as that; if they're sure of the actual place where the raid is to take place, they can send word and the Germans can make their defensive preparations accordingly. Quayle's in a position to find out what's happening. He's *persona grata* at all the Ministeries, and so are some of his men.'

'We could round up the whole mob, Quayle and his entire staff.'

'You're getting tired, Bill! The whole idea is to fox them, didn't you say it yourself?'

'All right, all right,' said Loftus lugubriously. 'But it's getting on my nerves a bit, Gordon.'

He was a long way from convinced that Mike would be all right: too often agents had gone out on lone missions and failed to return. The only records of that fact were in a card-index in Craigie's office, and in the memory of Loftus, Craigie, and those who knew the men and what they had done. Loftus brooded on that for a while, but eventually they went to bed.

Although Hershall remained in the next flat he sent no message that night, while by then the German radio was plugging the assassination sensation on every wave-length in Europe and the world.

The air quivered with rumours. Hershall was dead, or was dying. The Arch-Criminal of Europe had at last received his desserts, cried Hamburg; Hershall the War-Maker was dying, bellowed Radio Paris. On it went in a mounting crescendo, and as no denials were issued by the B.B.C. the tone of the Axis-inspired reports grew stronger and more circumstantial, the howl of joy which went up in Germany stretched to every corner of the world.

Next morning some of the reports were brought to Loftus's flat while he and Craigie had breakfast. They read them with increasing perturbation, and were fully expecting to be told abruptly by Hershall that the deception would have to stop, for the people in the streets were getting worried.

'Well, I can't say I haven't caused a stir,' said Loftus ruefully, later in the day. 'I'll begin to believe he's been hurt myself, soon. We should be hearing from Vichy any minute now.'

Quayle was back at the office.

He was closely watched, but did nothing to arouse suspicion. Towards the early evening, when he left the office, he was followed by two agents, but went straight to his Regent's Park home, and was received by his wife, a tall, majestic-looking woman and an admirable match for Quayle's large, florid, and portentous personality.

There was no news from Vichy at seven o'clock; the raid was timed to start at ten.

While Loftus and a dozen others waited on tenterhooks for word from Hammond or their confederates in France, the dapper Tallboys was talking to a farmer ten miles from Boulogne, a rumble of military transport filling the air. A hundred yards away, on the main road, a cloud of dust told of the movement of the column. Tallboys, whose mastery of the French language was indistinguishable from that of a native, and who, moreover, possessed a beautifully forged special permit allowing him to go within ten miles of the coast of Occupied France, let the farmer do the talking.

The farmer's hatred for the Nazis was ill-concealed, but not being sure of the man to whom he was talking he did not allow himself to utter it too openly.

'Sometimes, *M'sieu,* I think they are frightened, they move their troops so fast. Perhaps one day the English will come.'

'Who knows?' asked Tallboys, and shrugged.

'It will be a real fight this time, *M'sieu.'* The farmer watched his caller narrow-eyed, obviously suspicious that he might be yet another agent of the accursed Gestapo. 'I am told that the English now have great armies, and all the arms that they need.'

'We are told!' shrugged Tallboys. '*M'sieu*, it is for us to do what we are asked by our masters, and work ourselves until we are but bone, to sweat and never to curse, to go hungry and never resent a Boche eating too much. *Nom d'un nom*, what do they think we are? But—the day will come, *M'sieu*, the day will come when we shall show them!'

The farmer's eyes lit up.

'Well said, *M'sieu*! We are in full agreement, and who knows'—he looked towards the moving cloud of dust—'who knows that it will not be sooner than we expect? They are frightened tonight, the dogs, they will be more frightened at another time. Five thousand troops, not one less, have moved into the Boulogne area today, I swear it.'

'They have had word of an attack, perhaps?'

'Some dog of a spy.' The Frenchman spat. 'But it will not always avail them, *M'sieu*.'

Tallboys agreed, and left soon afterwards, travelling by train in an overcrowded carriage.

He would have been in good time to get to a radio-transmitting station where he could send word to Hammond but for a delay on the line while a troop train went through. Seeing it, Tallboys was more than ever convinced that the Germans were prepared for the raid, and he was desperately anxious to get word through to England.

He reached the transmitter at last, one in a small village near Arras. He travelled to the village by cycle from Arras station, and was four times held up by German soldiers who demanded to see his papers, which were reasonably safe from being suspect. Each delay put him into a greater ferment, and he was late when he arrived at the estaminet.

There were Germans in occupation, but almost the first thing that greeted him when he reached the cellar where the transmitter was built was a whispered:

'They have mostly all left, *M'sieu,* there is talk of the invasion starting tonight.'

'Talk!' exclaimed Tallboys. 'The Boche is ready for whatever is coming.' He threw his hat into a corner, sat down in front of the transmitter, sweating freely. He had some trouble in getting a reply from England, for the ether was jammed as he had not known it to be for months. He managed to make contact at last, and sent out his message in morse. He was starting again when he heard a thump upstairs, turned, and saw the little keeper of the estaminet standing quite still, his face deathly pale.

'They have found us,' he whispered, 'they have found us.'

Tallboys swung back to the transmitter, snapping:

'Hold them for two minutes. Two minutes!' He began to talk swiftly, no longer using morse. 'England, can you hear me? England, can you hear me——' he heard a faint response, just distinguishable amidst the confusion in the air, and hurried on: 'Attack expected—got that? Attack expected.'

The faint, ghostly voice of the receiving station came to his ears, and then was drowned by a rattle of machine-gun fire from upstairs. He heard the estaminet keeper cough and saw him stagger back, firing from an automatic even as he fell. Tallboys snatched a gun from his pocket, fired three times into the apparatus, smashing the valves. Then he jumped round as a figure in field grey appeared in the doorway, the gun in front of him.

Tallboys shot him through the chest.

As he fell another took his place, a machine-gun blazing. Bullets carved through Tallboy's chest and he hardly coughed as he slumped down, his hand gripping his automatic, his face splashed with his own blood.

As he died, a man in London was saying:

'Message from XL 201, saying "*attack expected*". Send word of that through at once, will you?'

'Yes, sir,' said an orderly smartly, and a few seconds later the telephone on Loftus's desk began to ring.

# Chapter 14
# Sacrifice For What?

Under the cover of the darkness, and helped by smoke-screens from small craft which swept close to the coast near Boulogne, the special troops landed. They went at speed and with a fierce determination, the greater because they knew that the attack was not a surprise. The covering fire from the defending positions was withering, cross-fire came from all directions, and dive-bombers began to scream above them.

As the invasion barges reached the shore the men, leaping from them, ran forward and flung themselves down to find some cover.

Above, the Stukas roared with ever-increasing viciousness, dropping their cargoes into the water and around the small boats, creating a hell upon the seas, turning the normal air men breathed to fire and smoke and death. The crackle of small arms, the bark of pompoms, the deeper note of the heavier guns farther inland, the flashing of the shells and the bright light of flares, the fierce red flame from the bombs, the streaking of tracer bullets: all were there, all part of the raging inferno of what a few minutes before had been a quiet stretch of beach protected only by barbed wire and, at some points, small concrete block-houses.

Beyond the coast the British 'planes were strafing gun positions, the great roars of the explosions of their bombs echoing above the nearer sounds.

Men with blacked faces and dulled buttons carrying automatic rifles and revolvers, crawled slowly up the beach towards the source of the inferno. Advance parties went forward with their hand-grenades, carrying death and destruction, knowing that they had to smash those defences or else perish.

So they crawled forward, or at least held on. The noise increased, the crescendo of the roaring engines and the crashing bombs deepened to an incredible intensity.

The order to withdraw came.

They lost men on all sides as they went back to the sand and then into the water.

Above them the air was filled with light, the clear shadowless light of flares, and the deep, ravenous light of the gunfire and the bombs. In such an unholy illumination the small craft could be seen, near the shore, waiting for the survivors. A motor torpedo boat maintained a fierce fire to cover the withdrawal of one party, and it seemed that a hundred guns were trained on it. The men at the guns kept on, but one by one they were put out of action until only one man remained at a pompom; he kept firing although the boat was holed a dozen times and sinking fast.

There was no relaxing in the shooting from the shore, no diminishing of the protecting fire from the warships further out at sea. The small craft were loaded and began to head for the larger vessels, men were in the water, swimming or standing up to their necks.

Farther out, crowded boats began to make for the English coast, with night fighters screening them from the air.

Soon a silence fell...

The word reached Berlin, and then was telephoned to a place known only to a few, where Hitler was receiving messages from many people. The megalomaniac who knew the answers to all the problems that arose. Following the rumours of Hershall's assassination and the ominous silence of the British radio, the news brought hope with it.

From Hitler's headquarters there went a call: '*Who brought the information of the coming raid?*'

In a small hotel near Laval's headquarters, a short man who was known to be English, and who had been to and from England frequently in the past few months, was sitting in an easy chair in a room overlooking a wide boulevard. Somebody tapped on the door. He looked round, removed his feet from the window-ledge, and called:

'*Entrez.*'

The Frenchman who entered was tall, thin, and melancholy, with a high, domed forehead from which fine streaks of hair grew well back. He was Monsieur Jules Traves, a barrister.

'Hallo, Traves,' said the Englishman, who, snatching what comfort he could, displayed his shirt-sleeves. Though his hair was grey, his face, now beaded with perspiration, was youthful. He looked up with a quick, winning smile. 'Now what's up?'

'I have just come from Laval, my friend. There is a great desire to find the man who brought the news of the Boulogne raid.'

'I didn't bring the news, I took the message over the radio.'

'Can you name the man who sent it?' asked Traves.

'No, and I don't propose to try.'

'I understand that Berlin requires a full statement of how the news is obtained. It is considered just possible that future information would not be so reliable, and——' Traves shrugged. 'You know the German thoroughness. I should not be awkward if I were in your shoes.'

For some seconds the Englishman stared at him.

'Now listen,' he said at last, I don't know who gets it or how it's obtained. The organisation in England is pretty good, and it does a fine job. I receive the news in Vichy, and pass it on. That's all I can tell you, except——'

'I am glad there is an "except",' said Traves with a tense smile. 'I should not like to hear that anything had happened to you, my friend.'

'It won't,' snapped the Englishman. 'If it does, there will be an abrupt end to any more red-hot news.'

'You forget your aptitude for boasting, M'sieu; you have often told me that if you had to run, then the news would be radioed to others.'

The youthful face of the Englishman no longer looked amiable. There was apprehension in his expression, and the perspiration which ran into his eyes looked almost like tears.

'There's a man who comes out to see me, he's coming the day after tomorrow.'

'Where will you meet him?'

'He'll come here.'

'What is his name?'

'When he gets here it's Hebas. In England it's Howe.'

'And when do you expect him?'

'Around seven o'clock the day after tomorrow.'

'And you think he will have information as to how the news is obtained?'

'He's my only direct contact with England,' said the other sourly. 'I can't make promises for him.'

'Of course not, of course not,' said Traves smoothly. '*Au revoir, mon ami.*'

He went out of the room as quietly as he had entered, leaving the Englishman frowning at the closed door.

Traves sat in a café, where, lingering over a drink, he could safely watch those moving up and down the street.

After a while a short, well-dressed man appeared, with waxed moustaches and an ostentatious air of satisfaction allied to a peculiarly covert expression. To the average Frenchman the word 'collaborationist' was written in his apprehensive manner and his obvious prosperity. The new-comer sat down.

They talked idly for a while, and then their voices dropped. In truth the little 'Frenchman' was Stewart, who had just come from Bruce Hammond.

Traves reported what he had learnt.

'Howe, Edward Howe,' mused Stewart. 'Nice work, Traves. How are you making out?'

'My friend, you need have no fears when the attack does start, from every village and every town there will be such an uprising as has never been seen! I almost pity the Boche.'

'Don't waste your time,' said Stewart grimly.

He stayed there for half an hour longer, and then left, casting a furtive glance about as he entered the street. He was shouldered off the pavement three times in a hundred yards by inoffensive-looking people who whispered '*Canaille*' into his ear, as they gave him a surreptitious push. He avoided any major scene, and eventually reached a large house in the residential quarter of the city. A card in the window announced '*Appartements*'. The front door was open. A sharp-faced woman was sitting by another open door farther along the passage, but averted her eyes when Stewart entered.

He went upstairs to a room on the third floor, opened it, and stepped through.

Bruce Hammond was lying in his shirt-sleeves on the single bed. His shoes were off, as were his collar and tie, and his brown hair was ruffled.

Stewart closed and locked the door.

'Something's breaking,' he said, and passed the news on.

'We're getting on. Any word about Tallboys?'

'Nothing.'

'I don't like the sound of it,' said Hammond. 'He would have sent word by now if he's all right. Well, I'd better get ready for the return trip.'

Some hour and a half later, when darkness was over the land, Hammond left the apartment house and cycled through the streets of the Vichy suburbs towards the open country. There was a new moon, and it gave enough light for him to see with reasonable precaution. Three times he was stopped by the police, but his papers were in order, countersigned by a high Vichy authority, and he went on without difficulty until he reached a tiny village called Auberne. About Auberne the land was very flat, and there were meadows which were ideal for landing-places for air-craft. Hammond made his way to the estaminet, drank poor white wine, and talked innocuously to the host. Then he went outside and entered the rear of the estaminet. A girl, little more than a child, admitted him.

'You were not followed, *M'sieu?*'

'All safe, *cherie*,' said Hammond cheerfully. 'And how is Yvonne tonight?'

'Well, as always, *M'sieu.* I am asked to send word to you that the aeroplane will be here at ten o'clock.'

'Good, that's fine,' said Hammond. 'I'll go out and wait for it.'

It was turned half-past nine.

Hammond walked towards a copse of trees near the village. No one else was about, and as far as he was aware no one saw him. He reached the copse, where he could hide until the aeroplane came to pick him up.

Then he heard the sound of an engine.

It was not that of the expected aeroplane, but of a car coming along the road. He moved a little so that he could see the beam of a headlight: There were three of them. They were coming from Vichy and travelling at high speed.

The cars stopped in the village, and the engines were turned off. He was too far away to see what was happening, although when lights shone from doorways and windows he caught glimpses of men moving. He heard a shout, and then another: then he saw the flash of a pistol shot.

He was standing rigid, looking towards the village. He saw that the door of the estaminet was open, and the figures of men in uniform silhouetted against the light. Then people streamed out. From the far end of the village there came a sudden shouting, an upheaval doubtless intended to distract the attention of the men who had arrived.

Hammond knew that the men were Gestapo agents, and assumed that there had been a rumour of the secret radio receiving set at the estaminet. He suspected that the village would rise as one man against the raiders; but he was afraid that someone would talk and give him away.

Then in the distance he heard the drone of an aircraft engine.

# CHAPTER 15

# QUICK WORK

The noise was so loud that Hammond knew that the Gestapo agents must hear it. He had expected to see the cars move off at any moment, but they were silent for a long time, although cries and shouts, oaths and curses, from the village proved that there was reason enough for it.

The village was fighting.

Hammond did not know that the rumour had been spread around that the English were sending for an agent, and that the Gestapo must not be allowed to get him first. There was hardly a man or woman who did not play some part in creating confusion, and as the Gestapo officers were in the estaminet three men fell upon the guards by the cars. That started the shooting, and was the herald of a burst of machine-gun fire which cut a dozen down and sent the others rushing for cover. The first car, freed of attackers, started off towards the copse of trees, and the noise of the aeroplane.

Hammond saw that the landing light of the aircraft was now so low overhead that the noise of its engine made the ground shiver, awakening the birds and sending them flying upward with shrill chatter.

He saw it touch land.

He ran swiftly towards it, judging the place where it would stop. The pilot knew his job to perfection, for he came to a standstill at a spot where he had a clear run for a take-off. The doors opened and a man stepped down, while Bruce shouted to him:

'Get inside, get ready!'

As he spoke the engine had been cut out, and his words travelled clearly. He heard the noise of the approaching car, also, and was desperately afraid that the others would follow and arrive in time to stop the take-off. He redoubled his speed, while the man who had left the aircraft returned, and the engine started again.

Hammond reached it.

A man was waiting to help him as he clambered on to the wing and then climbed through the door. As he tumbled inward a burst of machine-gun fire from the Gestapo car rattled out, bullets pecking the ground about the 'plane. The door slammed. The 'plane moved off, slowly at first, but with gathering speed. The driver of the Gestapo car tried to get in front of it, but the gunner of the aircraft loosed a single burst.

The car turned over; for a moment its headlights carved a way through the near-darkness and then went out.

The aircraft surged upwards, and a man said something to Hammond; he did not hear the words, for he was watching the lights in the village and could imagine what was happening there, could picture the savagery of the Gestapo who had been foiled at the very moment success appeared to be within their grasp. He knew that the little village would be a place of mourning and weeping for a long time to come.

Watching, he saw the lights of the village going out one by one; that seemed symbolic. He thought of the little receiving set in the cellar, specially built to take short-wave messages from England, and wondered what kind of an 'investigation' there would be. He thought of the pale face of Yvonne, and her burning enthusiasm, allied to a strange, fatalistic fear.

Then there was an explosion which burst red and ferocious upon the earth. It was in the centre of the village, and he had no doubt that it was at the estaminet. He was near enough even then to see pieces of débris flying upwards above the flames, which settled down to burn and keep burning. Hammond watched while the flames grew smaller, and the height of the aircraft increased.

'Bad show, eh?' a man shouted into his ear above the roar of the engines.

'A bad show, yes, but a damned heroic one. What a people!'

'Who?' The speaker seemed surprised.

'The French,' said Hammond, and shrugged. 'Who else?'

It was barely midnight as he rang the bell of Loftus's flat, and when the door opened he heard voices coming from an inner room, Hershall's among them. Loftus himself opened the door and smiled at Bruce, whose arrival had been heralded by a telephone call from the aerodrome. His expression altered as he saw Bruce's face in a better light.

'Anything wrong?'

'We can't use Auberne again,' said Hammond shortly. 'Any news from Tallboys?'

'No, and I doubt if there will be. He had to use English when he sent word over, and that meant an emergency.' His face was set. 'Have you got anything?'

Hammond related what had happened. He omitted no details, and finished:

'Traves knew that Vichy was getting the dope, of course, and he's been looking out for some time. It's an odd business. This Englishman in Vichy, a fellow named Smith, gets word from England. He's the receiving end, and he says he knows nothing of how it's done over here. Smith sells the information to Vichy, and I gather Vichy sells it to Berlin. The thing is, Bill, they don't know anything about the business except that "Smith" gets radio reports from, presumably, England, and collects the money. Then this man Howe, Edward Howe, turns up in Vichy from time to time and collects the cash. Presumably he brings it back to England and there's at least an even chance that he knows where the information comes from. Know anything about him?'

'He was killed, or rather he killed himself.'

Loftus explained more to Hammond who was aghast at the news. The information that the man was dead wrecked theories which had been comforting him all the way from France.

All the time the mutter of conversation came from the next room. Hershall's voice predominated.

'So that is that,' said Hammond slowly.

'There's something else, Bruce. Mike Errol went down there two days ago and then disappeared. He was with a brother of Edward Howe, and I've had photographs of the couple—they're twins, and they look like it. A pretty good likeness.'

'Where's the brother?' snapped Hammond. 'There's just a chance that he'd do.'

'We haven't found him yet. And we've something under forty-eight hours to fix it.' He ran his hand through his hair and then stood up. 'Come on, let's pass it on to the others.'

When they entered the further room, Hershall was saying:

'And if the public can take what they've already taken, I can't imagine that they're going to be so badly affected by the rumour that I'm hurt.'

'If only you realised how great an uplifting effect you have on them,' commented Laidlaw. 'If only——'

'Now look here,' said Hershall brusquely. 'If anything happened to me I'd be replaced in a few days, and in a few weeks, even if I weren't forgotten, the people would be working and fighting and arguing and criticising, just as they have with me. Anyhow, I'm not going to die yet.' His eyes creased at the corners as he looked at Loftus and Hammond. 'Now we've started this, we need to keep it up for a few days more. If it's bolstering up German morale, all right—let it.'

Laidlaw shrugged his shoulders.

Craigie said quietly:

'One of the chief anxieties is whether the raid the other night should have been allowed to go on. The view in some quarters'—he eyed Laidlaw frankly—'is that it was an unnecessary sacrifice. Over a hundred and fifty men were lost.'

Loftus said slowly:

'I think we can prove that it was worthwhile, gentlemen.' He smoothed back his hair and was aware of the quick gaze from all the others. He went on to explain Hammond's news, and Hershall's eyes were very bright when the story was finished.

'So they not only feel sure that they are getting wholly reliable information, but we know part of the organisation which is selling it.'

'We'll do more,' said Loftus briefly. 'If we can get hold of this brother of the man Howe we've got the thing in our pockets.' He went on quickly before anyone could interrupt: 'Both the Howes speak French fluently and German fairly well, both know France, and the Vichy and Berlin authorities have never seen Edward: so his brother would be more or less assured of getting through. The only contact necessary for him in Vichy would be a man named Smith, and we can handle Smith quite effectively.'

'You don't even know whether the brother is alive,' snapped Laidlaw.

'We will soon,' said Loftus gently.

There was not a lot more said, and Hershall and Laidlaw went into the next-door flat by the concealed communicating door. When they had gone, the three leading men of Department Z were left alone together.

Hammond broke a short silence.

'Everything depends on finding Mike Errol and Howe.'

'If there's no result by the morning, Bruce, will you go down?' asked Loftus.

'Why not tonight?'

'Because it won't take much longer if you wait for the early train,' said Loftus, 'and you can get some sleep. You'll stay here for the night.'

They went to bed soon afterwards, Loftus insisting on having the alarm clock, and promising to call Hammond in good time for the early train.

On the next day Hammond went down to Radstock, and thence to Lashley; and on this day, also, things began to happen to Ainsworth.

Loftus's first knowledge of it was a telephone call from Regina, to say that Ainsworth had left the flat and was

obviously in a badly worried frame of mind. The second
was a telephone call from the agent watching Lannigan's
house. Ainsworth had gone there, and what was the agent
to do?

# CHAPTER 16
## MANY THINGS AT ONCE

Martin Ainsworth rang the bell at Lannigan's Queen Street house.

Ainsworth had no idea that Rita lived there.

The encounter with Lannigan on the Chelsea Embankment had been simmering in his mind. He was unable to find a reason why the man should offer to help him, and the mystery of the chance meeting worried him. He forced his uneasiness aside as the door opened and the ugly man who dressed so well and whose voice was so unexpectedly mellow smiled at him.

'Good morning, Mr. Ainsworth, I'm glad to see you.'

'I thought perhaps—I mean, you suggested that I should call on you,' said Ainsworth. 'I hope that——'

'Do come in,' interrupted Lannigan, 'this way.' He led him to an overcrowded, musty drawing-room. 'We don't need to beat about the bush, Mr. Ainsworth. I know that a thousand pounds is difficult to find, and I think we might be able to come to some arrangement. About Quayle, now—neither of us have any liking for him. You worked for him for some time, of course, and you will know something about his habits, his daily visitors, his usual haunts.'

Ainsworth felt a kind of mesmeric fascination at the smooth suavity of the voice, although he disliked the trend of the questions.

'Do you know, Mr. Ainsworth, whether he was ever associated with a Colonel Ratcliffe?'

'I think he knew such a man, yes.'

'Or a Mr. Edward Howe?'

'He did know a man named Howe, certainly,' said Ainsworth.

'Excellent,' murmured Lannigan. 'Excellent. Now I think we had better go upstairs, Mr. Ainsworth; I have some papers there which I think will interest you. In a very short while we shall know whether we can work together successfully, and if we can, then I can assure you that my principal will be only too glad to assist you in the matter of current expenses.' Lannigan's ugly face widened in a smile. 'After you, sir. Straight up the stairs.'

Ainsworth went up a long, narrow flight of stairs and paused on the landing.

'You need to go up the next short flight,' said Lannigan. 'The door on the right. Excuse me.' He pushed past Ainsworth, who stood surprised, even bewildered, but was not aware of anything to make him afraid, although his heart was beating fast. Even when Lannigan unlocked the door and ushered him into a pleasantly furnished bedroom, obviously a woman's room, he was only puzzled.

He did not know that it was Rita's home.

'I find it necessary to keep important papers in the least expected places,' said Lannigan, and pushed an easy chair forward. Ainsworth sat down and accepted a cigarette. Lannigan went to a drawer in a dressing-table, unlocked it, and drew out a cash-box. First he lifted a bundle of treasury notes, then a number of crisp banknotes. He put them carelessly on the top of the dressing-table, and if he saw Ainsworth's eyes turn towards them he made no comment.

He took some other papers out, and then said softly:

'I think that Sir Edmund Quayle is not only a liar, and a slanderer and a cheat, Mr. Ainsworth, but it is possible, just possible, that he is an agent of the Nazis.'

Ainsworth's eyes turned from the money. He stiffened in his chair and looked into Lannigan's still smiling face.

'I don't know where the devil all this is getting to,' he snapped. 'I believe a lot of things of Quayle, but I don't think he's a spy. The names I have affirmed as knowing him are only of social acquaintances.'

'Gently, gently, Mr. Ainsworth, your loyalty does you credit. Now you may or may not be aware that the young lady who has taken a flat opposite you in Chelsea, and who has been so friendly and so kind, is an espionage agent. A spy. Her attentions to you have been so devoted because she thought that you could give her certain information of importance.'

'What utter rot!' shouted Ainsworth.

He stood up abruptly and stepped to the door. His movement surprised Lannigan, who followed swiftly gripping his arm. At the same moment Lannigan put his hand to his pocket, and drew out a small knife with the blade opened; the handle of the knife was wrapped in a handkerchief. All Ainsworth saw as he wrenched himself from the man's grasp was the handkerchief.

Then Lannigan stabbed him.

He plunged the knife into Ainsworth's back, aiming for the heart. It was a powerful, swift, and dastardly blow, but all Ainsworth felt at first was a sharp stab of pain, white-hot but not acute after the initial spasm. It made him stop pulling at Lannigan, and he looked into the man's face, saw the thin lips drawn tight over large white teeth. In a sudden panic he raised his voice and tried to shout, but Lannigan clutched his throat and the shout died away into a gurgle.

Ainsworth stood quite still by the door, his head turned, staring at Lannigan.

Lannigan drew the knife out, and then stabbed again.

This time Ainsworth gasped, for the pain was much greater. He felt as if his very vitals had been torn, and there was a deep, horrible thunder in his ears. Lannigan's face looked distorted, his grin was a leer, an ugly, bestial thing.

Then there was a sound at the window.

Ainsworth did not hear it, but Lannigan did, and turned abruptly with the knife poised for a third thrust. Lannigan saw the head and shoulders of a man outlined against the glass.

He stood quite rigid, staring, and then realised that the man was standing on a ladder. He saw a hand move, and snatching up a book from a table by the bed he flung it at the window.

The glass broke into a hundred pieces: the figure ducked, and for a moment was lost to sight.

Ainsworth slipped to the floor with a groan. By then Lannigan was at the dressing-table, whipping up the notes. He thrust them in his pocket and then turned and ran out of the room; he heard the crack of a bullet and the lead peck into the wall behind him. He was unhurt, but in the violence of his haste barely saved himself from falling down the stairs. He gasped for breath, but recovered himself and plunged on. He was desperately afraid then that there would be someone waiting for him by the door, but there was no one there and the door was closed.

He wrenched it open and ran into the street. He was on the pavement when he realised that he held the knife and the handkerchief in his right hand. He flung them into the house, then turned and hurried away. A taxi drew near and he hailed it. The cabby stared at his pale, strained face, but said nothing. He accepted the order to go to Hampstead Underground station.

Lannigan sank back in the taxi with perspiration streaming down his face. He looked through the small rear window as the street disappeared from his sight, and saw a man turn the corner and run in the wake of the cab. A second taxi was in sight, and the man jumped on the running board.

Lannigan tapped on the glass, and when the driver turned his head, exclaimed: 'Faster, I'm in a hurry!'

The cabby trod on the accelerator, but the taxi behind held on. Lannigan expected to be shot at any moment, but suddenly saw the other cabby swerve to avoid a motor-cyclist. The delay was brief, but enabled Lannigan's man to get ahead.

Lannigan stopped him when he was round a corner, near Shaftesbury Avenue.

'I've changed my mind,' he said. He paid the man generously, then jumped out of the cab and slipped into a narrow side street. He hurried along it, past bombed buildings and plots of land which had once been the sites of imposing premises, turning right and left, until he felt sure that he was safe from being followed. Then, and not until then, he went to an underground station; he left the train he took there at Hampstead Heath.

At a kiosk near the station he called Mr Smith, and that hearty gentleman's voice rang warmly in his ears.

'Ah, my dear fellow, I have been expecting word from you. Has everything gone off according to plan?' Smith rumbled into a laugh.

Lannigan snapped:

'No. Ainsworth's gone, that's all right, but I was seen. We can't fix it on the woman, and Queen Street's closed up.' He heard a gasp from the other end of the wire as he hurried on: 'Ainsworth hadn't any idea about Q, and the others, except that they knew one another; he wasn't lying, he just didn't know.' He stopped, gasping for breath. Then: 'He can't have told the girl anything, it's okay.'

'All right.' Smith's voice was harsh. 'Now get away.'

'I'm going fast,' said Lannigan. 'Don't forget—Queen Street's closed up.'

He hung up abruptly, then straightened his tie and smoothed his hair before stepping out of the kiosk.

He saw several men lounging at the entrance to the station, but not until two of them approached him, one from either side, did he realise that they were police or special branch men. They put their hands on his shoulder, and one said jauntily: 'We'll have a word with you, sonny.'

Martin Ainsworth lay on the floor of his wife's room, half-conscious.

Lannigan's attack had not killed him outright, and he had even been aware of the shooting, and the noise, as a man jumped through the window in Lannigan's wake. He did not know, of course, that two men had been watching the house, and that one had followed Lannigan in a taxi while the other had joined the chase on a motorcycle, thus keeping Lannigan in sight all the time and ensuring his detention.

He did not know that Lannigan was being taken to Loftus's flat.

He only knew that there was a sharp pain in his back, near the heart. It frightened him. For some minutes he lay there with the uncomfortable pain and oozing warmth in his back; then laboriously and with the help of the door he pulled himself to his feet, He swayed from side to side; his face was bloodless, but he set his lips and went into the passage.

The house seemed empty.

Thought of the stairs brought a wave of nausea over him, but he went slowly towards them, and managed to get down the first four, the short flight Lannigan had mentioned. At the head of the main flight his head swam, but he gritted his teeth, pushed one foot forward, and then began the gradual descent.

He was thinking of Regina Brent, whom he knew as Regina Grey. He was thinking, too, of what Lannigan had said about her. His thoughts were confused, but he experienced a deep sense of disbelief. He did not think Regina Grey was a Nazi spy, he could not credit it. He felt that he was dying, and that he would not be able to keep on his feet for long, but he wanted to see her: he felt desperately that he had to see her.

He reached the foot of the stairs.

His head was filled with a fierce pain, a throbbing which grew worse with every movement he took. His eyes were half-closed, and all he could see at first was a sheet of dazzling white light; that cleared at last, and he could discern the open front door and the street beyond. He went out, not looking either way for some minutes, while several cars and tradesmen's vans passed him. His head steadied a little, and he turned it in one direction. He saw a taxi approaching, and raised his hand. The man stopped by the kerb, and Ainsworth gasped:

'Chenn Street—Chelsea. Number—11.'

'Right, sir.' The cabby peered at him narrowly. 'You all right, sir?'

'I'm—sick,' gasped Ainsworth. 'Must get—home.'

The cabby jumped down, and helped him into the cab. Ainsworth could not sit back in the seat but stayed on the edge of it. The jolting of the taxi sent agony through him, but he retained consciousness until he reached Chenn Street, and the cabby stopped.

"Ere, I'd better 'elp yer,' said the man sharply.

Ainsworth gasped his thanks. He knew that he could not reach the top floor on his own, and he had to get there; every second he had been in the cab he had been seeing Regina's eyes and face; and he had been hearing Lannigan's words: '*She's a spy, she's a spy, she's a spy.*'

He reached the top landing.

With an effort he took some silver from his pocket and paid the cabby, who rang the bell of Regina's flat as Ainsworth tried to touch it. There was no immediate response, and the cabby frowned and rang again. A stir of movement inside preceded Regina's appearance at the door.

She stopped abruptly at the sight of Ainsworth's white face.

'I've brought 'im 'ome,' the cabby said. 'Better look after 'im, missus, 'e's in a bad way.'

'Yes,' said Regina quietly. 'Yes. Thank you.'

She took Ainsworth's arm. He stood swaying for a moment, then leaned heavily against her and allowed her to lead him into her flat. The cabby went downstairs, and Regina pulled a chair towards Ainsworth and helped him to sit down. She did not know where he was hurt, but the look on his face told her that he was not far from death.

He said: 'Miss—Grey. Must—tell you.'

He drew a deep breath and then stopped.

For some moments there was silence, and Regina was wondering where he was hurt and whether she could help him. It seemed to give him great pain to move, but he kept still and was breathing much more steadily.

'Not long—to live,' he said. 'Listen—Lannigan—man I went to—to see. Said you were—a spy.'

Regina drew a sharp breath.

'Wonder—whether—you are,' gasped Ainsworth. 'Not—enemy agent—anyhow. Listen. Lannigan wanted to know—about Quayle. Friends of Quayle. Listen. Quayle sees a lot of—man named—Ratcliffe. Visits him—often. I told Lannigan—that—he didn't. But he did. Often. And a man named—Howe. Disturbed them at—at a conference, once. Why Quayle—fixed me. Reason for the quarrel. Never trusted—Quayle. Been watching him, trying to find—what he does. But remember—Howe. Ratcliffe. Dang'rous men. They frightened Quayle. Badly frightened. Know they did. Listen.' He paused a moment, and his breathing grew worse. Only strength of will kept him going for the few moments of life that were left to him. 'Listen. Quayle goes to Ratcliffe. Underground—workings. Colliery. Near—Bath. Pit closed—down. I kept—kept quiet about it. Didn't know the reason. Anyhow, needed—money. Bad thing to do. All bad, have always been bad.'

He paused again, and Regina spoke for the first time: 'Don't worry now, Martin, don't worry.'

'Can't—help it. Married that shrew of—a woman. Ruined me. Ruined me.' He paused, and then drew a deep breath. 'But I wished—it was—different. Loved her, once. Not the way—I love—you.' His eyes were suddenly clear as they stared into hers.

'Rest now,' said Regina softly.

'Going to rest—for a long, long while.' Ainsworth's eyes widened, his hand suddenly gripped her wrists. 'You've been—a wonderful——'

As he spoke his lips parted more widely, and his grip relaxed. He fell heavily against the back of the chair, shuddered involuntarily, and then lay still.

Regina rested Ainsworth as well as she could, bringing up another chair to support him. Then she stood aside and stepped to the telephone. In a few seconds she was repeating to Loftus the gist of what had been said, and Loftus promised to be at Chenn Street within twenty minutes.

In the intervening time, she washed her hands, and kept out of the little room where Ainsworth lay dead. She could not prevent herself from thinking of the way he had spoken of her and of his wife.

Then Loftus arrived.

She repeated what he had told her, while Loftus found the keys in Ainsworth's pocket and opened the man's flat. He searched amongst papers there while Regina continued to tell the story, calling it to mind almost word by word.

He smiled at her, and his manner helped to keep her steady.

'The disused coal mine. There aren't many mines in the Radstock area, and we know about the Howe Colliery, which was closed down. Mike and Howe are probably down there.'

'*Mike!*' exclaimed Regina, and the intensity of her words made Loftus look up at her sharply. 'Why didn't I know? Where did he go? Why——'

'Easy,' said Loftus. 'We'll get him before the show is over.' He straightened up from a desk, shaking his head. 'Ainsworth didn't keep any records of it, but I don't see that it matters. Colliery's disused. I suppose the Ministry of Mines will know something about them, and we'll want blueprints and an ordnance map of the district.' He seemed to be talking more to himself than to Regina, but that was deliberate, for he was watching her closely, surprised at the effect that the news of Mike's disappearance had on her.

He lifted the telephone and dialled Craigie's office. Craigie promised to contact the Ministry of Mines for the necessary information, and then said quietly:

'Oh, Bill. Lannigan has been picked up. He's in the middle of talking. He arranged the attack on Hershall, and the spreading of the rumour. He's given us the address of several agents up and down the country, and implicated "Smith"—but the similarity of names is just coincidence, this Smith isn't any associate of the Vichy one, or so it seems. Lannigan and Smith are working direct for Berlin. They've had orders to try to find who's getting the Commando information and putting it through. But what about coming over and seeing him yourself?'

'I'm on my way,' said Loftus, and then quickly: 'And I'm bringing Regina with me. Give us a quarter of an hour.'

# Chapter 17
# Trek To Somerset

In the Department office were Craigie and a jaunty, broad-shouldered, small man, and with them Lannigan.

Lannigan had broken down completely after his detention, and his story was complete when Loftus arrived. Berlin had started Lannigan and Smith on the work of checking, not satisfied to get the information from Vichy, but anxious to have complete confirmation.

Lannigan admitted that key-agents up and down the country had been ready since the beginning of the war, doing nothing which would attract police or Home Office attention, waiting only for the right moment to begin their activities. The attack on Hershall was to have been the first of many; others, on various ministers, would have followed at intervals.

The spy's ugly face, so much at variance with his well-cut clothes and mellow voice, was set in an expression of fear mingled with an anxiety to talk freely in a desperate hope to save himself from hanging or a firing squad. His anxiety to make a statement was nauseating.

'You have had orders from Berlin, you say, to trace the source of the leakage?' snapped Loftus.

'Yes, that's right.'

'And the purpose of that is to get the information to Berlin direct from you, and thus check it with the information sent through Vichy?'

'That—that's right.'

'And you'd got as far as knowing, or suspecting, that Quayle was mixed up with it?'

'He is, I tell you!' snapped Lannigan. 'He won't deal direct with us, we've tapped him a dozen times. He won't touch us, but he gets the dope and passes it on to Ratcliffe and Howe. I *know* he does. Howe went out of the country at regular intervals. He had a permit to leave the country; I think Quayle fixed it, but I'm not sure. We had him followed. He always left a few days after the Commando raids, and went to Vichy. He made contact in Vichy with an Englishman named Smith. He collected the money Vichy paid for the information, and brought it back here.'

'Now what about Ainsworth? Why were you so interested in him?'

'Loftus, is—is Ainsworth dead?'

'He's in a bad way,' said Loftus evasively.

'I—I shouldn't have attacked him. It was all worked out by Smith, my Smith. He reckoned if we could get Ainsworth at Queen Street, and kill him in his wife's room, it would look as if his wife had done it. The idea was to kill him with a paper-knife she uses. It had her prints on it, and he would have been found in her room. She'd carried out some small jobs for us and she was getting curious. We couldn't afford to take chances with her. She didn't know enough at the time to do any damage, but——'

'All right, go on,' said Loftus crisply. 'You were telling us why you wanted Ainsworth killed.'

'We wanted to get some news from him. We knew he'd had a row with Quayle, and all about the libel and slander case. We thought he might know something he hadn't dared use in court, and planned to find out what it was. We—we offered to help him with cash, he was up against it when the damages and costs were awarded. But—but he was too long coming. We found out that he didn't know much, we only wanted one or two little things confirmed. We did plenty of checking up on Ainsworth. We searched his room, and we were watching from there one day when he was out, that's how we learned that—that she'—he looked towards Regina—'was spying on him. She made contact with one of your fellows, I knew the man, and that settled it. Anyhow——'

'Actually you were afraid we might learn from Ainsworth what you couldn't learn yourself,' said Loftus slowly. 'That's why you decided to kill him. All right, go on. You arranged the murder, planning to get his wife framed for it. Wasn't her row with a man in the Cherry Club contrived by you?'

'Yes, yes, I'd forgotten that. I'm telling you everything, I'd forgotten it! We arranged that she would shout about murdering Ainsworth, to strengthen the case, and we framed the quarrel at the Cherry. One—one of our men started it. He was a man who'd contacted Ainsworth earlier; Ainsworth was friendly with him at one time.'

Loftus said: 'The gentleman dresses as a lieutenant, and he's a friend of Colonel Ratcliffe's.'

'Yes, that's right, his name's Ellison. He—he's no soldier, he's one of us.'

'And what's he doing with Ratcliffe?' demanded Loftus.

'You don't need telling that,' snapped Lannigan. 'He's made contact with Ratcliffe, and he's trying to find out what Ratcliffe does with Quayle. That's all.'

'All right, we'll say it is,' said Loftus more crisply.

Craigie looked at the jaunty Department Z agent.

'Take him to Cannon Row, Ted, will you?'

'Right you are,' said 'Ted'.

The door slid to behind them.

The hearty Mr. Smith, who had imagined himself to be playing so important a role while being perfectly safe from suspicion, had been arrested half an hour after Lannigan, and was then waiting for interrogation, He was brought to Craigie's office by two large young men who seemed to have no thought of anything but cigarettes and eyeing Regina, whom they clearly admired.

Smith was a shivering jelly of a man. His dark hair was awry, and the white streaks of the cranium showed vividly. His laughter was gone, his heartiness completely dissipated. His hands trembled every time he moved them, and he could not keep his knees from shaking. It was obvious that he was completely bewildered by the trend of events, and could not convince himself that he had been caught.

With him there came a report that his house was being thoroughly searched, and that already the names and addresses of the 'assassination agents' were being discovered. The police would go into action at once, and a threat to the safety of the leading politicians was being removed even before its seriousness was fully realised.

What was more important, Smith not only confirmed everything that Lannigan had said, but gave details of the radio contact he had with Germany.

When he had gone to Cannon Row, to await further interrogation, Craigie said quietly:

'We'll maintain his contact with Berlin, I think.'

'How do you mean?' demanded Regina.

'They'll expect to hear from Smith,' Craigie pointed out, 'and they may as well continue to hear from him. It'll convince them that everything is in perfect order, and that's exactly what they want to hear. A continued policy of making the enemy happy,' he added with a slow smile. 'We're not doing badly, Regina.'

'I can't keep track of it,' confessed Regina. 'It seems fantastic that it's all happened since—since I saw Mike and Mark. What would have happened if I hadn't told them about Father?'

Loftus shrugged his shoulders.

'Who knows? We might have made as much progress, but I don't think it's likely. The problem is, what's going to happen now?' he added thoughtfully. 'I wonder how long those maps and blueprints will be?'

Craigie telephoned the Ministry of Mines, to be told that a messenger was on his way with them. Craigie went out of the office, and the doors were closed behind him as Loftus pressed one of the buttons beneath the mantelpiece. Regina eyed the buttons, her expression startled, although she had seen them operate several times before.

'Does everything work by electricity, Bill?'

Loftus grinned.

'A lot of it! When I first saw the gadgets Gordon uses and knew that he had sliding doors and this-and-that, I thought it was all highly coloured shop-window dressing. But it works, and that's what matters. There aren't a dozen people in the building who know this office exists, and except for half-a-dozen of us, no one can get in from the outside. Gordon's gone to collect the stuff from the Ministry, from an outer office. All part of the "keep 'em mystified" policy.'

As he spoke, a green light showed in the mantelpiece. He pressed a button near it, and a part of the wall slid open. Craigie entered, carrying maps so voluminous that he had difficulty in squeezing with them through the door.

With him was a short, slim man dressed in morning clothes, pale-faced, deferential. Craigie introduced him as Cartwright, a specialist in blueprint and map reading.

'Good man,' said Loftus briefly. 'Now let's have a look at things down at Lashley.'

They spread the maps and blueprints over Craigie's desk, and Cartwright pored over them with Loftus and Craigie. Regina stood by the fireplace where a small fire burned despite the warmth of the day outside.

Cartwright was saying:

'If the two gentlemen disappeared about here, sir'—he indicated a point on the ordnance map with a pencil—'then they disappeared immediately above some old working of the Howe mines. Not workings used in the lifetime of the present Howe family, but——' he peered at a blueprint—'workings which were closed as far back as 1849. I see from the particulars here that the workings were wrongly prepared in the first place, and led to the side of this—er—escarpment, perhaps, would be the best word. And the colliery which used to be fairly near is now completely gone. Shafts—they were shallow at that time, please remember, no more than a few hundred feet, and often not so deep—were drilled in several places. There is one here close to the edge of the escarpment.' He went into details quickly, and plotted the course with a pair of minute compasses. 'There is no evidence that it was filled in, although others nearby were. These old prints are never absolutely accurate, mind you, and subsidence will often alter the whole appearance of old mine workings. But, roughly speaking, there was an air shaft about—here.'

He marked a spot on the ordnance map; it was less than a hundred yards, by the scale of the map, from the position of a summer house, clearly marked. The larger building of Lashley Cottage was there, also, with Beddiloe House a little to the west and, on the lower ground below what the specialist in map reading called the escarpment, was the house of Mr. Hanton.

'Good,' said Loftus. 'Can you be ready for a trip to Somerset in an hour?'

'Yes, sir,' said Cartwright, without batting an eye.

'Good man. I'll meet you in Whitehall outside the main doors at—' Loftus looked at his watch—'twelve o'clock exactly.'

'Very good, sir,' said Cartwright, following Craigie as he released one of the wall sections. When the door had closed, Loftus passed a hand over his hair and said slowly:

'A pleasant little bloke, and he'll be useful. The trek to Somerset seemed indicated, Gordon. All right with you?'

'I was going to suggest it,' admitted Craigie. He filled his meerschaum, and then added quietly: 'What are you going to do, Regina?'

She hesitated for a moment, eyeing his amiable countenance, seeing that he appeared to be quite free from anxieties or concern for Mike, or, indeed, anyone. She drew a deep breath and then said slowly:

'*Are* you human? Don't you realise that Mike's been missing now for forty-eight hours? *Forty-eight hours!* Can't you understand what it means?'

Craigie spoke quietly into the ensuing pause.

'We're more used to this kind of waiting than you, and that makes the difference. You see, Regina, individuals don't matter. If it's possible to find Mike we will find him, but as far as our objective is concerned, Howe is far more important.

He might play a vital part in deceiving the enemy, and—our job is just that. Just that,' he added softly, but his expression was bleak, and it seemed to Regina that she suddenly understood how deeply this man felt, how much, in fact, his men meant to him.

Regina said in a low voice:

'I'm sorry. Will—will I be in the way if I come down?'

'No, Gina, but you will be if you're late. Come on, let's get some things packed.'

Regina had just time to go by taxi to her flat, and pack a small case. There was a policeman standing outside Ainsworth's door, and she wondered whether the body was there, or whether she would need to see it again.

It was gone, but a heavily-built and large man, whose sandy hair and moustache had a peculiar look of having been dusted recently with flour, was in the room. He introduced himself as Superintendent Miller, and she eyed him curiously, knowing that he was the liaison officer between the Department and Scotland Yard. His face was impassive, and he gave an impression on first acquaintance similar to that which Loftus created.

As they stopped outside the Lion Hotel in Lashley village, Regina saw two men. One was tall and narrow, clad in grey, immaculate to the point of excess. But for a long, thin nose he would have been good looking. His eyes were dreamy, and he looked faintly bored.

By him was a shorter man in a flannel suit, fair-haired and smiling brightly. Both of them stepped forward.

Loftus introduced them quickly as Wally Davidson and Young Graham, then asked: 'Anything developed?'

'Nor a bally thing.' Davidson took a slim cigarette case from his pocket. 'Not a thing, Bill. We saw Pat last night. He's getting restive; all Ratcliffe and this other bloke—Ellison, isn't it?—do is to sit around in the garden, play a spot of golf—good-looking course not far from here—and this and that. Absolutely a rest cure.'

'Any others of our boys here?'

'Haven't seen 'em,' said Graham.

'Meaning who?' asked Davidson.

'The fellow on Quayle's tail,' said Loftus. 'The only man who seems to do nothing at all suspicious is Suspect Number 1, or Quayle in person.' He lit a cigarette which Davidson had offered, and then added slowly: 'Something must turn up sooner or later, but at the moment our job is to find Mike.'

'We've been looking for him for twenty-four hours, drat you,' said Davidson.

'Useful police fellow here named Webber,' put in Graham. 'He's been doing all he can, but——' he shrugged.

'We've something that might help,' said Loftus. To Regina they still seemed appallingly casual. 'Where's Bruce Hammond?'

'Haven't seen him,' declared Davidson. 'Didn't even know that he was coming down here.'

Regina was looking at Loftus, and she saw a change in his expression which amazed her. His casualness and non-chalance was gone completely, his eyes hardened and his chin thrust forward.

'He should have been here by half-past eleven, and he was coming direct to this pub.'

'He hasn't shown up,' Young Graham said slowly.

Only then did the change in Loftus's expression convey real meaning to Regina. She experienced something of the cold dismay which Loftus felt.

He said quietly: 'So we're looking for three of them.'

It proved that Davidson had travelled down with Graham in a Lagonda, and they climbed into their car, which was further along the road, and followed on to Lashley Cottage. At the gates of the drive they saw a uniformed policeman, and a tall, clean-limbed man in plainclothes. To Loftus, Davidson said: 'That's the Inspector johnny, Webber.'

'We'll rope him in, Loftus.'

They collected Webber, who asked few questions, and then went as far as they could by car and walked the rest of the way up the hill to the summer house and the wonderful view beyond, with Cranton's Heath House bathed in the afternoon sun.

Cartwright and Loftus approached the summer house together.

# CHAPTER 18
# DISCOVERIES UNDERGROUND

To Mike and Brian the few hours following their descent into the old shaft had been a nightmare.

For what had seemed an interminable time they had gone on through the darkness, until they had come to what appeared to be a dead end.

They had continued to walk about in the darkness, however, testing the walls, beating against them with their clenched hands. The all-pervading gloom had made their plight worse, while they had begun to feel the first pangs of hunger, pangs accentuated by the fear that they were trapped and would not see the light of day again.

And then they heard voices.

Neither of them had spoken, both had kept still and rigid as they listened. They heard a man's voice saying: 'They must be about somewhere.'

'Probably they're drowned,' someone else suggested.

The floor where they were waiting was dry, but until that moment the blackness had been impenetrable. Suddenly they could see the disc of light shining from a torch, and against the light they saw two men, walking slowly as they flashed the torch to and fro.

Mike and Brian crowded back against the wall, but knew that if the torch was flashed their way, they would be visible.

The footsteps drew nearer, the light growing so powerful that it hurt their eyes. Then abruptly:

'*There they are!*'

There was something wrong with him, Mike thought, he had not taken out his automatic, resting in the hope that they would not be seen.

Brian Howe stirred.

Mike gripped his arm.

'*There they are!*' the man shouted again, but did not move towards Mike or Brian, but towards the other side of the spacious underground chamber in which they were standing. The light showed them both, grotesquely shadowed, bending over the figure of a man stretched out on the floor.

'Keep quite still,' Mike urged in a whisper so low-pitched that he wondered whether Brian could hear it. In any event Brian made no attempt to move, while the two men bent lower over the outstretched body.

The speaker said in tones of sharp surprise:

'It's Blaney!'

Mike caught his breath: Blaney, whom he had wounded and whom Brian's brother had tried to run down, the man who had escaped and evaded the police. Small wonder he had succeeded in that, but why was it that he was there, apparently unconscious?

Voices were low-pitched and barely audible after that, until one of the men lifted Blaney and began to carry him. Mike gripped Brian's hand, and together they followed. The noise of their progress was covered by that of the men ahead and the heavy breathing of the one carrying Blaney.

Soon, a different light percolated through to them.

It was not daylight, but a diffused glow from an electric bulb. The little party ahead of Mike and Brian were shown clearly, and they could even see Blaney's head lying limply over the first man's shoulder.

It came through a door which led, it seemed, into a wide room. They could see chairs and tables, and the electric light softened by a shade which would have looked well in any living room. A smell of cigarette smoke reached them.

They drew nearer.

Mike was watching the door. He saw that it was a heavy one, but there appeared to be only an ordinary lock on it. He discovered that much when the others went through, and the door closed. Although it was shut they could hear voices, and one of the men said clearly:

'How is he?'

'He'll come round,' the second man said. 'Banged his head, I shouldn't wonder. That's why the police didn't get him.' A pause, and then: 'He'll know what happened to Howe and Peterson.'

'The police got *them*,' said the first speaker harshly.

'Don't you believe it, Howe wouldn't let himself be caught.'

Brian was clutching Mike's wrist: for Mike it was easy to understand something of what the other was feeling, but it was not in the forefront of his mind: he was thinking of that room beyond, of the fact that the search for them had been temporarily postponed, and that there was only a simple lock on the door.

He pressed his ear close to the keyhole.

He heard the key turn in the lock, but that did not worry him. There were various sounds, and they waited for what seemed a long time. Then there was a groaning noise, and a sharp question:

'Can you hear me, Blaney?'

A grunt, and then another question:

'Where's Howe?'

Very softly, only just audibly, Blaney's reply came:

'He—ran away. The—swine, he—tried to run—me down. Killed—Peterson.'

There was a gasp, and for a few moments silence in the room. Brian's hand, gripping Mike's arm, seemed like a steel vice.

'If I ever get my hands on him——'

'Take it easy, take it easy,' said one of the others softly. 'You'll be all right. How's your arm, does it hurt?'

'Hurt! Why it——'

'We'll give you a shot to send you to sleep,' one of the men said quietly. 'You'll be all right as soon as you come round. We'll have a doctor look at that hand, too, it's getting dirty. Easy, now.' There was another pause, and a tinkling sound. Then a gasp, presumably from Blaney. Another wait, and one of the speakers uttered a low-pitched laugh.

'He's gone all right.'

'Poor fool,' said the second man callously.

'He served his purpose,' said the first.

The only sound which followed was of footsteps and then the closing of a door. Silence fell.

After a long wait Mike slid his hand into his pocket and drew out a bunch of keys, one of them long and slender, having a small piece at the end at right angles to the main stem. He pushed it into the lock, and there was a faint clicking. That lasted for a long time, but no other noise broke the silence.

A sharp tinkling sound on the other side of the door made Brian jump.

'I've pushed the key out,' said Mike softly. 'We won't be long now, provided the beggars don't come back. Are you carrying a gun?'

'No.'

'Take this one,' said Mike. He pushed his automatic, re-loaded since the shooting on the road, into Brian's hand, and then concentrated on picking the lock. It took a long time, but at last the lock clicked back.

He turned the handle, and the door opened. They stepped into the room with bated breath. It was dark. Standing still for a moment, Mike whispered:

'You go right, I'll go left. Keep to the wall, and grope for a switch.'

They started slowly. A dull sound was followed by a soft oath as Brian stumbled against some object, and all the time the shuffling sound of their movements was audible.

Then: 'Got it!' Brian exclaimed, and pressed down the switch.

The light which flooded the room was so bright that it not only dazzled them but hurt their eyes. For a moment they could not see, and stood facing one another, their eyes narrowed. It was a full minute before they were able to pick out items of furniture. Blaney's body was on a settee in a room furnished like a lounge.

Brian drew a deep breath.

'So they did kill him.'

'Shot of morphia, probably. There's the puncture.' Mike looked at a round, red spot on Blaney's forearm, and then added as he glanced at the swollen, discoloured wrist: 'I think he would have been in a bad way anyhow. I shot him two days ago and the wound's gangrenous. I wonder how the deuce he got down here?'

After a while, they decided that it would be better to put the body outside in the tunnel, and did so quickly.

There was a small room adjoining the larger one. Modern plumbing was too much to expect, but there were two barrels of water standing by an enamel bowl, towels, soap, and everything they required. They washed in turn, expecting to hear sounds of approach at almost any time, but no interruption came.

A search disclosed a stock of tinned food, water and sweet biscuits, and some boxes of cigarettes. The provisions were in a cupboard in the wash-room, and as they opened some of the tins with a tin-opener obligingly handy, Mike grinned across at Brian, whose tension was also easing.

'This isn't going to be so bad.'

'At least we'll be fed,' said Brian.

To their amazement there were no interruptions for the rest of the day. They knew the time from a small clock ticking on a cabinet in the room. The ventilation was excellent, and towards midnight Mike won, by the toss of a coin, the privilege of being the first to sleep. They arranged that he should be called at three o'clock.

Mike took his spell on watch, and let the younger man sleep until eight o'clock. To him the prospect of getting out seemed bright, but it dimmed when he found that the door leading into the unknown was proof against his efforts. He tried everything, even shooting at the lock, but could not make the door budge.

'So we just have to wait,' commented Brian slowly.

They waited for the rest of that day and went through another night, still taking turns on watch. Nothing transpired, and the morning of the next day dragged past. They opened more tins, and had finished a snack meal when Mike looked up at Brian with a crooked grin, and said:

'Taken by and large, we're not doing too well, Brian.'

'We're doing damned badly,' said Howe sharply.

That was about the time that Loftus was driving between the grey walls and houses of Radstock, and nearly an hour before Loftus and the others started for the summer-house.

Mike was lighting a cigarette, and Brian filling a pipe with tobacco taken from cigarettes in the store which was large enough to last them for several weeks, when they heard a sharp noise outside. They stopped abruptly, and stood up. Mike approached the door, his gun in his hand. He stood behind it, while Brian waited near him. Instinctively they realised that if the door opened their one chance was to attack swiftly; whoever opened the door would see and smell the smoke, and know there was something amiss. They waited tensely, and then a key grated in the lock.

'Wait for it,' Mike said steadily.

There were four bullets left in the gun, and he was wishing then that he had not wasted any on the lock. He watched the handle turn, and saw the door open. The man who entered was obviously pushed violently, for he sprawled into the room and struck against a chair.

It was Bruce Hammond.

Brian Howe exclaimed aloud. There was a split second of startled silence, and then the man outside ripped out another oath and pulled the door shut in obvious alarm. Hammond was in Mike's way, and prevented him from getting to the door: it closed with a bang, and the key turned in the lock.

Hammond sat up dazedly.

Brian drew a deep breath, and exclaimed:

'That pretty well finishes us. They know we're here.'

'Easy,' said Mike. 'There's a long time yet, and the fact that Bruce is here suggests that the other boys aren't far away.' He put out a hand and helped Hammond to his feet, then said with absurd gravity: 'Lieutenant Brian Howe, Mr. Bruce Hammond.'

Hammond's clothes were rucked about him, his face was dirty, his hair dishevelled. Slowly and deliberately he straightened his coat.

'Well, well,' he said. 'We've got half the country out looking for you, and you're making yourselves at home here. I came down to join the other searchers, and struck someone I didn't expect to see. I followed 'em, and they came into an old colliery working. I got too close, and they shanghaied me. It's as simple as that,' he added, but then went on quietly: 'They'll get on to us soon, but I think we've a fifty-fifty chance.'

'We can use it,' said Mike. 'When did you get back from Vichy?'

'Vichy!' exclaimed Brian sharply.

Bruce leaned back in his chair and regarded the young naval officer thoughtfully. Although all of them knew that there was a chance of an assault coming from outside at any moment, and knew that the assault would be in force, none of them appeared to be thinking about it, all were more concerned with other things. If Mike kept to a position in which he could see the door and be sure that it did not open unexpectedly, neither of the others seemed to notice it.

'What the deuce do you mean by *Vichy*?' insisted Brian.

'I've a story to tell you,' Bruce told him.

The telling took a little more than twenty minutes. In the beginning it did no more than astonish Brian, but as talk of his brother's periodical visits to Vichy to collect the blood-money was broached, he lit a cigarette and stared bleakly at Bruce, who, making no attempt to dramatise his story, slowly approached the subject of using Brian in place of his brother.

'There's a certain amount of danger in it,' he said. 'You don't need telling that. But the fact remains that the Boche believes that your brother can tell them just how the leakage is arranged, and they want to contact him. There's no evidence yet that anyone knows he is dead, and in any case no one in official quarters in Vichy or Berlin will be able to be sure whether you're yourself or your brother. What do you think of it?'

'I'll do it, if it can be done,' said Brian slowly.

'You'll get a thorough briefing, of course,' said Hammond. 'When we get out of this dump we can arrange that. Mustn't forget to let the Admiralty know, either!' He smiled fleetingly, and then added in a voice low-pitched and suddenly impressive: 'It's difficult to assess the importance of it, Howe. We can fox the Boche if it goes through all right. We can convince him that we're striking on the continent at a certain spot, and get started at another before he knows the news is false.'

Brian drew a deep breath.

'It—it's hard to believe.'

'Anything unusual always is,' said Bruce, and smiled again very briefly. 'Bill Loftus is fond of saying that it's difficult for the individual to realise that everything can depend on him at a given moment. A hell of a lot depends on you, Howe—little short of an easy success in landing in France.'

Brian swallowed.

'I suppose I'm not dreaming.' He paused, and then went on in a sharper voice: 'But we haven't much chance of getting out of here. They'll come at any time——'

'Don't play your luck too low,' said Hammond. 'The others are about, and what I struck at the first go, the others will find in good time. I wish——'

He stopped abruptly, for there was a sound at the door.

Mike moved then, going so quickly that Brian started as he passed him. Mike pulled an easy chair forward and jammed it under the door, pressing it home and grunting:

'We ought to have thought of that before, but it will serve.' He grinned. 'More the merrier, folk, and remember we've a back way out if it really comes to a push.'

'Where?' demanded Hammond.

'The other door's open, isn't it? We don't exactly want to withdraw,' he added quietly, 'but if it comes to it we can fox 'em in the workings. There are a brace of torches on that cabinet, you'd better grab one apiece.' He waited, but although they expected the door to open and the effort made to push the chair away to start at any moment, nothing transpired.

'There *was* a noise,' Brian said softly.

'Don't I know it,' whispered Mike. 'I don't like the show a bit, it's getting uncanny. It could be a nerve-war,' he added half-jocularly; and then he sniffed.

His head went up, and his eyes narrowed. He stared towards the door for a moment, then approached it and went down on his knees. He did not speak until they heard him say:

'Geraniums.'

'Geraniums!' exclaimed Brian. 'What the devil are you doing there? Get up! I——' he paused abruptly, and then turned to Hammond, his voice taking on an entirely different note. '*Geraniums!*' he repeated softly.

'Smell thereof,' said Mike rising to his feet and backing slowly. 'They're pumping lewisite through to us. Not a bad idea, but they can't fill the whole workings.' All of them went towards the second door and opened it. The smell of geraniums was growing stronger, and Hammond started coughing and could not stop. They went outside and closed the door behind them. There was a faint chance that they would not be gassed; they saw none at all of getting out.

# CHAPTER 19
# BOTH ENDS MEET

Although one of the two torches was on, the darkness seemed to drop upon them. They could imagine the hiss of escaping gas, and what it would be like in the room which had so lately given them harbourage. They did not stop to think of the men who had loosed the gas and tried to kill them: they thought only of the slim chance of their own safety.

They went forward slowly but steadily.

'All in all, it's about what we had to expect,' said Mike. 'The odds aren't so good as we made out, Bruce. The beggars will know what we've done, and come after us. Not much doubt of that.' He sniffed. 'No geraniums here, anyhow.'

'How far ahead is the water?' asked Brian.

'Another couple of hundred yards, I'd say,' said Mike. 'Listen for it.' They reached a corner, went round it, and then waited. They heard shouts from the far end of the tunnel, by the room they had left, and then the clear report of a shot reached them.

'Shooting to make certain,' said Mike. 'Not long now.' He grinned briefly. 'Well, we can rely on the others to spike Quayle's guns, and stop the leakage. Half a loaf is better than no bread. I wish,' he added a little too casually, 'that we had three loaded guns apiece instead of one and four bullets.'

Neither of the others spoke.

There was a silence which seemed to last for a long time, and then they heard footsteps. Sounds travelled far in the underground passage and were deceptive, but they knew that the hunt was up, that it would soon be a case of retreating as far as the water, and it made little difference whether they went back so far or stayed here and fought it out.

Mike said again:

'We could try a sortie.'

'I've been thinking just that,' said Hammond slowly. 'Howe, you count in this show, we don't. When the shooting starts try to get through them. Just run for it if the light's too big for you to keep in the shadows. We'll draw their fire.'

Howe said nothing, but grunted.

'Go to Bill Loftus, 55g Brook Street,' said Mike casually. 'He'll know all about you. Failing that, ring Whitehall 4141, and ask for him. Now this is important: spell your name backwards.'

Brian said in a harsh voice:

'Loftus, at 55g Brook Street, or Whitehall 4141, and if I ring there I have to spell my name backwards.'

'Nice work,' said Mike. 'He'll make quite a boy, won't he, Bruce?' He stopped as the footsteps drew nearer, and a glow of light showed. He peered round the corner, and then drew back swiftly. 'Here they come, wait for it.'

The crash of a shot spat out, reverberating round and about the tunnel, bringing down chippings upon their heads. They waited tensely while the noise of approaching men drew nearer. Mike held the gun, then went down on his stomach and squirmed into the main passage. The light from several powerful torches shone on him. He fired at one of them before shots came his way, and the glowing orb went out.

'One,' he said *sotto voce*.

He felt as cool as he sounded. If he could put the lights out in time to give Howe a slim chance of escape among the attackers, that was all that mattered. Odds-against chances had to be taken, there was none other. He wondered in a vague, detached way whether it was possible for them to break through, when a new noise came, the sharp stuttering sound of a tommy-gun. A wave of bullets swept across the mouth of the tunnel, but the aim was too high.

He fired again, and missed.

He drew back, and his lips were twisted wryly. There was, now, not even a slim chance; at their slightest movement the attackers would again open fire with the machine-gun. He felt a queer sense of frustration, and wondered what the others were thinking.

*And then a low-pitched voice came from behind them.*

'Friends or foes, folk?'

Upon Bruce Hammond and Mike Errol there fell a sudden silence, an abrupt blanketing stupefaction of amazement and incredulence. Brian Howe swung round, seeing only the darkness, while the low-pitched, rather tired voice repeated:

'Friends or foes, and I don't think it's foes. That you, Mike?'

'Wally!' exclaimed Mike hoarsely. 'Wally, by all that's holy. *Wally!*'

'Hush, I've heard you,' said Wally Davidson, his voice in no way flurried. Across his words there came another stuttering roar from the tommy-gun, but that faded into silence and he added: 'Not nice people, are they? Is Howe here?'

'Ye-es,' said Howe uncertainly.

'Hop back,' said Wally. 'Straight along, and you have to go through a spot or two of water. Keep your head high! Someone's at the other end, and a rope's dangling down from the summer-house. Good climbing.' He paused as Brian hesitated, and then spoke with a touch of impatience. 'Get off, man, you matter.'

Brian turned and walked hesitantly along the tunnel.

Davidson put out a hand to touch Mike's shoulder, and then discovered that Bruce was there. Another burst of machine-gun fire followed, and after it Wally said:

'I wish we'd brought one, we'd teach the beggars something. Only one rope back there, so far,' he added inconsequentially. 'Your turn next, Bruce.' He gave a whisper of a laugh. 'You matter, too!' He paused, and then added: 'Loftus said Howe first and you second, if I found you. Young Graham's standing in the water, which you doubtless know of. Mike, I'll toss you for the next place.'

'Done,' said Mike.

'And that reminds me,' said Davidson. 'Intervals of three minutes. They've sent for another rope, by the way.' He showed the illuminated dial of a wrist-watch, and said: 'You go off in a couple of shakes, Bruce. Where's that penny, drat it?'

As another burst of machine-gun fire came along the tunnel, he turned his torch on to a handful of coins, selected one with some difficulty since both hands were full, and put it between his lips. As Bruce Hammond started off unhurriedly Wally tossed the coin and caught it: it glittered in the light of his torch.

'Heads,' called Mike.

'Heads,' said Davidson a moment later. 'Nice calling, Mike.'

'You go next, and no arguing,' said Mike quickly. 'It's been my show, and I'll see it through.' He grinned widely, and then went down on his knees again and loosed a burst of fire from another gun which Davidson had brought.

The answering volley from the machine-gun proved that he had not put the gunner out of action.

He had seen enough, moreover, to show him that the attackers were approaching slowly, and they were no more than fifty yards from the corner. Mike thought grimly that they would come in a greater hurry if they knew of the escape hole.

'Better keep 'em busy,' said Davidson. He peered round the corner and sent two more shots towards the lights of the other party. He scored a hit, for one torch went out and an eerie cry as of pain travelled along the tunnel. The remaining torchlight showed a bright oval on the wall, for the corner represented a 'T' junction; and it grew gradually brighter.

Seconds dragged, and yet surprisingly soon Davidson's time of departure arrived.

He went off at a leisurely rate, while Mike remained at the corner, seeing the glow of light from the torch growing larger all the time. He felt fascinated by it, knowing that if it grew too close it would be the end of what little chance remained to him, but that if he stepped into sight and fired at it, the tommy-gun would probably finish him in one burst.

He had Wally's watch, and glanced at it. Thirty seconds had gone.

He thought he heard whispered voices from the tunnel, and his heart began to thump. The torchlight was so brilliant that he could see his hands and his clothes. He put the muzzle of his automatic round the wall, and squeezed the trigger; the answering fire came so quickly that a bullet struck the nose of the gun and wrenched it from his fingers.

At the acuteness of the pain he gasped, and let the gun clatter to the ground. There was a profound silence immediately afterwards and then he heard the whispers again, and shuffling footsteps.

A minute and thirty seconds had passed.

To Mike it seemed that he might as well have to wait an hour as a minute and a half, but it did not occur to him to hurry in Davidson's wake. He heard heavy breathing then, while rubbing his wrist and backing a few paces. Without the gun he was helpless unless he could take refuge in the darkness. He thought of the water, which would slow up his progress, as well as that of the pursuers if they ventured into it. There was at least a chance that if he reached the water the others would assume that he and his fellow prisoners would drown.

Then he saw a distorted shape on the wall, a grotesque shadow which chilled him. As he watched it growing larger his heart beat so fast that it seemed to echo about the tunnel. The whispered voices followed, and then he felt easier, for he realised what the shape was: the men attacking wore gas masks.

He backed further away.

Except that he had to go slowly, he did not think of time. The slower he went the greater the chance the others had of getting up the rope, although he was by no means sure that all of them would get through: once they realised that his only gun had gone the attackers would get bolder.

He stumbled when his foot went into the water.

He remembered vividly all that had happened from the time he had first fallen into the stagnant pool; and then he turned his back on the attackers, a necessity which cost him dear, for there was something horrible beyond words in expecting a bullet in the back. The feeling grew worse when the light played on the water in front of him, and he heard the crack of an automatic; at least the tommy-gun wasn't yet in play. He floundered forward until the water reached knee-level, and then plunged into it bodily. He was not exactly swimming, for his hands and knees kept touching bottom, but he presented a more difficult target.

Then he wondered whether he could hope to get through, for bullets skimmed the water, while chippings fell sharply from the roof and from the sides. With the noise thundering in his ears, ten times louder now that he was immersed, he struggled on. His ears were drumming, his heart beating fast, but nothing struck him, and presently he heard a voice not far ahead.

'Right, Mike!'

His heart seemed to turn over in relief.

'Graham here,' said Young Graham. 'The others are up—ah! Here's the second rope!' Something splashed into the water near Mike's face as he managed to get a foothold. He was only dimly conscious of what was happening, except that the shooting seemed further away. He felt Graham thrust a rope into his hands and heard him snap:

'Tie it around your waist!'

Mike obeyed, his hands trembling and fumbling. As he made the knot he felt the rope jerk. There was a pause, and then he was lifted from the water and felt himself swaying to and fro in the shaft. Once he swung against the side painfully, then knocked into Graham, who was being hauled up on the second rope.

Neither man spoke, neither man could see, except that the light at the top of the shaft, only a pinprick from the bottom of it, grew gradually clearer. At last Mike discerned Graham's face, turned upwards, while from below them there were rumbling sounds, none of them distinguishable.

'More shooting,' he thought. 'They're trying to fire up the shaft.'

The daylight above him was so strong then that he had to close his eyes. He heard voices, and someone said:

'One more heave. Now then—one—two—heave!'

With an upward surge he was taken out of the shaft and over the edge of the summer-house floor. He did not see the crowd gathered near, policemen and Home Guards as well as Loftus, Hammond, and several others. Davidson was standing by the edge, while someone bent down to help Mike up.

'You're all right,' said Brian Howe. 'You're all right— Good Lord, I can hardly believe it! I——'

Howe stopped abruptly, for someone else drew near. Mike turned towards the newcomer, his eyes so unaccustomed to daylight that he could not properly see her, although he knew that it was a woman.

'Mike,' said Regina. '*Mike!*'

'Gina!' He shot out his hands and felt her responding grip as firm and eager as his own. For a moment they held hands and he burbled something he did not properly understand himself. Regina laughed. Her eyes were gleaming and he stared at her incredulously, unable to believe the message in her expression.

'Gina!' he exclaimed.

'Friends,' said Loftus dryly, 'no time for interludes of *tendresse*. Plenty later, maybe, but for the moment we've got a job to do. Mike, take Brian to Lady Beddiloe's, will you? And you go with 'em, Gina, to vouch for the scarecrows!'

'Where are you off to?' asked Mike suspiciously.

'The entrance Bruce discovered,' said Loftus. 'We want to close it up. Nothing for you just now. Our job's nearly over, but look after Brian Howe as if he were a crown jewel.'

Mike took a short step forward as Loftus, Hammond, some of the police, Graham and Davidson started off. He had no desire to stay behind, except that he did not want to lose sight of Regina. But it was Regina who held his arm, thus keeping him back, and he shrugged his shoulders.

He started with the others to walk to Beddiloe House with a bodyguard of policemen and Home Guard. At the nearest point that a car could come into the grounds of Lashley Cottage, one was waiting, and he clambered into it with the others. He was on edge to have word from Loftus, not knowing where he had gone or what had been discovered. He remembered that Bruce Hammond had talked of seeing someone he had not expected, someone who had guided him, unwittingly, to the entrance of the old mine. At least Hammond would know where it was.

But what about Quayle?

And what of Ratcliffe and the thin-lipped man, whose name he did not know. He had glimpsed the thin-lipped man once, but had never seen Quayle or Ratcliffe. Odd business, not knowing the people you were fighting.

The car pulled up outside Beddiloe House, and he climbed out, helped Regina down, and suddenly stopped worrying about other things. He was about to say something foolish, prevented himself, hugged her shoulders with one arm, and then turned towards the door.

Regina stopped short, while Mike stared at the tiny creature who stepped on to the porch, a lovely lady in a flowered dress whose eyes lighted up at sight of Regina.

'Rita Ainsworth,' breathed Regina. 'What on earth is she doing here?'

# Chapter 20
## Considerable Progress

Although Mike had seen a photograph of Rita he did not recognise her until he heard Regina's exclamation, and saw her startled expression.

The question found an echo in Mike's mind, while Brian Howe looked at the little woman in some bewilderment. Mike's thoughts were swift, as Rita hurried down the steps and reached Regina, holding out both hands and gripping the other girl's.

She breathed: 'Where is he? Oh, please tell me, where is he?'

Regina drew a deep breath.

'Who—who do you mean?' she asked, and Mike saw that she was playing for time in an effort to collect her thoughts before answering the question.

'Oh, please don't pretend,' said Rita quickly. 'If only you knew how sorry I am for what I've done. I—I know what a beast I was to you the other day, but you must believe me when I say that I was excited. The main thing, the only thing that matters, is, where is he? I must see him!' Her fine, bold eyes were staring tensely at Regina, and Mike—not knowing that Ainsworth was dead—wondered why Regina was so taken aback. 'If only I can make him understand how sorry I am, and what a fool I've been!'

Regina said slowly:

'We'd better go inside.'

'Oh, why must you be so unkind?' demanded Rita hotly. 'I know I was beastly rude to you, but I wasn't myself, I tell you. I'll apologise, I'll do anything you wish, but tell me where Martin is. I must see him!'

Regina repeated: 'Let's go inside.' She went forward, and Rita followed her.

Mike and Brian stared at them and then at one another. The naval officer shrugged his shoulders, as if saying that it was beyond his comprehension, and then they followed the girls.

In the spacious hall, so steeped in tradition, Lady Beddiloe was standing by the drawing-room door, trim and delightful to look at, charmingly vague as to what was happening, but with her blue eyes showing understanding and compassion. Even Rita's tension eased a little at sight of her.

She came forward with a hand outstretched towards Mike.

'Michael, I *am* glad to see you. But my dear boy! You must have a bath! And—why, Brian! I didn't recognise you. I'll tell Harris to get baths running at once, and——'

'Leave it for a few minutes, Aunt Bess, will you?' Mike's voice was a little strained. 'I think I need to talk to Regina and Mrs. Ainsworth.'

Regina turned to him swiftly.

'Mike, leave this to me, will you? We won't be long.' Her glance succeeded in conveying a message which made it clear that she was really serious. A little uncertain, but anxious to do nothing to perturb Regina, Mike shrugged his shoulders and forced a smile.

'Right! And a bath isn't such a bad idea, eh, Brian?'

'Not bad at all,' admitted Brian.

'Ah, here is Harris,' said Lady Beddiloe. She gave instructions to the butler quickly, with details of the room they were to have and orders that some clothes be found for them, and arrangements made for the clothes they were wearing to be cleaned. She did not fuss, but the orders flowed so smoothly from her tongue that events seemed easy and natural.

Mike and Brian went upstairs, Regina and Rita into the drawing-room. As Regina entered it, Lady Beddiloe asked: 'You won't want me, dear, will you?'

'Not for a little while, thanks,' said Regina.

She closed the door, appreciating the older woman's thoughtfulness, but more concerned with the task ahead of her. Whatever she might have thought of Rita Ainsworth, she had come to the conclusion after the visit to Chenn Street that the woman had been in love with her husband; only love could have explained such an intensity of jealousy.

Breaking the news of his death would not be easy.

'What are you holding back?' demanded Rita swiftly. Her breathing was laboured, her voice held more than a hint of anger. 'What are you so secretive about? There *is* something between you and Martin, I was right, I——'

'Please be quiet,' said Regina. She brushed her hair back from her forehead, and her expression kept Rita silent for a moment, although her eyes were filled with suspicion and her hands clenched. 'This isn't going to be easy, Mrs. Ainsworth, and it will be a shock.'

'What do you mean, a shock?'

Regina hesitated. Further evasion would serve no purpose, and the tension was growing unbearable. She had suffered from the strain of waiting for news of Mike more than she realised, and it entered her mind that someone might have had to break similar news to her about him.

'What is it?' snapped Rita tensely. 'Where is Martin?'

Regina said quietly: 'I wish I hadn't to tell you this, but he died yesterday.'

There it was, as blunt as it could be but perhaps kinder because of it. She saw Rita's eyes narrow and then widen. The other woman backed a pace, clenched her hands and raised them to her breast. She did not speak immediately, although her lips parted and then closed several times. The room was very silent, except that birds were chattering outside, making a background of sound to this strange, almost macabre interview.

Then Rita emitted a low-pitched breath before she exclaimed: 'You're lying to me.'

'I wish I were,' said Regina.

'But you must be; he was as well as I am, he was perfectly all right when I saw him!'

'Yes,' said Regina with an effort. 'He was—killed.'

Rita backed another pace, struck against a chair, put a hand down to steady herself. Her lips were working, her eyes grew suddenly very bright. The quiet between them lasted for a long time, until Rita spoke in a lower, steadier voice.

'Who killed him?'

'You know the man,' said Regina. 'Lannigan.'

'Lannigan didn't know him.'

'He did,' insisted Regina, wishing that she could tell the other more, but uncertain how much Craigie and Loftus would want her to say. She went on, as Rita made no comment: 'Lannigan wanted some information from your husband,

and didn't get it. So he killed him. Lannigan is under arrest now, in London.'

It was then that Rita broke down, turning blindly to the window and beginning to cry, staggering towards a settee and falling on to it, burying her face in her hands and uttering sobs which racked her body, and which Regina could do nothing to help. Regina stood looking at her, feeling deeply for her, yet amazed that she was so strongly affected.

For the next half-hour Regina forgot that Loftus and the others were on an urgent mission of inquiry, and that Mike was upstairs bathing and changing. Nothing but Rita's crying seemed to matter, and the paroxysm did not seem to be nearing its peak but threatened to go on and on indefinitely.

Bruce Hammond and the others went through the village to the other side, up a short hill, and then across the fields of a farm, the house of which was old, picturesque, and well-kept, like everything on the Beddiloe estate. Bruce and Loftus did most of the talking, and amongst other things Bruce said:

'There's probably nothing much in it, Bill, but I saw her walking along here, and followed. I lost her and went up past the farm to a little cottage, and was shanghaied there. The cottage is just beyond that copse of trees,' he added, and glanced at Chief Inspector Webber. 'Do you know it?'

Webber rubbed his chin, and a constable, the local Lashley constable, said quietly:

'I know it, sir. Belonging to Lashley Cottage. Mr. Edward rented it out to a friend.'

'What's the name of the friend?' asked Loftus.

'Smith, he did say.'

'It's all "Smith" in this business,' growled Loftus, not in the best of tempers. 'What was he like?'

'Tall and thin,' said the constable, 'and with a big moustache and a beard. An artist, I heard.'

'Does he stay here often?'

'Not so often as all that, sir. Friends of his do come and go, especially since the bombing started. It isn't every week. Sometimes there be only one staying, and sometimes five or six.'

Loftus and Hammond exchanged glances.

'A useful place for a rendezvous,' Hammond commented, and Webber looked uncomfortable.

'I've never heard anything about the cottage,' he said. 'Edward Howe wasn't here often, Gregg, was he?'

'Not very often, sir, no.'

'No fault of yours,' said Loftus, answering the unspoken apology in the policeman's words. 'The question is, why did Rita Ainsworth come here?'

No one answered him, and they went on towards the copse of trees.

As well as Loftus, Hammond, Webber, Davidson, Cartwright and Graham there were six members of the Lashley Home Guard and an equal number of policemen. Near the copse and out of sight of the cottage, they gathered together, and Webber gave brief instructions to the men. A small party of four started off to round the copse and cover the cottage on the other side, while Loftus looked crookedly at the Ministry of Mines expert, who was sitting in the car and poring over blueprints and the ordnance map. The man's insistence on the existence of a shaft near the summer-house had launched a miracle; Loftus had considerable respect for him. As the party of four disappeared, Cartwright looked up and said eagerly:

'This cottage is near another shaft off the old workings, Mr. Loftus.'

Cartwright went into a wealth of technicalities which, though impressive, added little to the general knowledge of the others. But they were convinced; and they knew in any case that through the cottage where Hammond had been shanghaied there was a way to the workings; for Hammond had been taken there, and the kidnappers had certainly not gone through the village, nor far away; the whole district had been too well covered by police and Home Guards working the hunt for Mike and Brian.

'How long do we need to allow the others?' Loftus asked Webber. 'Ten minutes?'

'Twenty would be wiser,' said Webber. He looked a little nervous, an unusual thing for that cool and collected police officer. 'I hope we're in time,' he added, 'but there's no sense in showing ourselves too soon, and we must have it covered from all sides.'

'That's right enough,' admitted Loftus. He lit a cigarette, and then said more quietly to Hammond, Davidson and Graham: 'I've had some strange experiences, but this is queerer than any of them. Who are we going to attack?' He drew deeply on the cigarette and added: 'Ratcliffe? Quayle? And then there's a man whose name keeps cropping up, Hanton of Heath Place. A bit of a mystery, with plenty of money, and living right in the middle of the show down here. And what was Rita doing in this locality?'

'I couldn't say one way or the other about Rita,' admitted Bruce. 'She was in the village, and I lost her not far from here, but——' he shrugged his shoulders, and then stopped abruptly, to glance towards the copse. His expression made Graham and Davidson move their hands to their guns, Davidson with a speed of which he did not seem capable.

'Someone moving,' Hammond said swiftly. 'I wish—well I'm damned!'

Out of the copse and making no attempt to hide himself came the mountainous Best. The sun was shining on his untidy hair, his coat was rucked up, and there was a tear in the right leg of his trousers. His beaming face suggested that it was the grandest encounter ever, and as he drew nearer he rumbled:

'I thought you were a crowd of villains, drat you, and you turn out to be white-headed innocents. What's doing?'

'What are you doing?' demanded Loftus pointedly.

'Duty, old boy, just duty,' declared Best. He reached them and held out his hand. 'Spare a cigarette, Bill, I've run out.' As Loftus handed him his case, Best went on: 'Following the little lady, the way I was told, that's what I'm doing. Or I was.' He paused long enough to light a cigarette and then added: 'Bless her heart, I left her at Beddiloe House. Quite a time she's had. Inquiring all over the place for Regina Grey, and of course no one knows a Regina Grey, they all know Regina as Brent.'

Loftus said quietly: 'Let's get this straight, old son. You followed Rita down here from Town, and she's looking for Regina?'

'That's right,' rumbled Best. 'She called at several houses asking the way and making inquiries, while I remained a shadow and kept watching. Then she cottoned on to the fact that Regina's a Brent and not a Grey, and went up to the house. I saw she was in good company, as Mike and another cove were just arriving, so I left and came over here.'

'How did you know we were here?' demanded Loftus.

'I can see the cottage from the house,' said Best promptly. 'It's on a rise, y'know, and you'd be surprised what I saw. Wally looking as tired as ever, and I couldn't miss the

Lagonda. There's the place for things to happen, I thought, so here I am. How are tricks?'

'We don't know,' admitted Loftus. 'This may or may not be a way to the end of the hunt.' He glanced at his watch. 'Those twenty minutes are up, Webber.'

'I was just going to say so,' Webber told him. 'We can move now.'

The Home Guards and the police spread out on either side, making a semi-circle some two hundred yards from point to point before approaching the cottage, which came into sight as soon as they were past the copse. Loftus and the other Department Z men were in the middle, with Webber. Two Home Guards were left in the rear, to guard against the possibility of a flank attack.

The strange thing to Loftus was that there was no certainty at all that they would get results or even meet opposition. He felt not unlike Mike Errol had done, but realised more vividly than Mike the importance of finding the leaders of the organisation. They were not Nazis, if Lannigan and Smith were to be believed, but Englishmen betraying their country.

He could not believe that Quayle was not numbered amongst them, but that was only a vague, passing thought. The cottage was small, creeper-clad, and set against distant trees, which grew close to the edge of the hill. A mile away to the right was the summer-house whence they had come, and if Cartwright were right, the cottage was close to another shaft leading to the old, useless workings.

Loftus was thinking: 'It's all so easy that it can't come to much. I don't like it.'

The silence about them was disturbed only by the chattering of the birds and the rustle of a slight wind through grass already tall enough for a second cutting. The sun shone on the polished windows of the cottage, on to the rose-covered porch and the creeper-clad walls. The quiet worried Loftus, because it seemed to him that there were all the hallmarks of a trap.

Then, behind them, came the sharp stutter of an engine.

It came so quickly that at first they thought a machine-gun was being used, and Graham and Davidson flung themselves to the ground while snatching their automatics from their pockets. Loftus turned; Hammond and Webber followed his example. Down below, on a narrow track leading from the road, they saw a single motorcyclist. He was coming at reckless speed. The ridges in the fields sent the motor-cycle lurching right and left and a dozen times in as many seconds it appeared that he must be thrown. The rider kept in the saddle, however, while the little party stared towards him.

The Home Guards and the police went on, and suddenly there came a shout from the nearest guard.

Only Hammond turned, of those near Loftus. There was shouting, and he was in time to see a small round object curving through the air. It was a long way off, not near enough to do them any damage, but it dropped near the Home Guards, each man of whom flung himself to the ground.

The dull boom of an explosion followed; a gust of wind from the blast was felt plainly.

'Grenades or bombs,' Hammond said briefly. 'They're in there all right, Bill. Look out, here's another.' Hammond and Loftus this time saw the Mills bomb which was flung from the cottage towards the attacking guards, and Webber shouted:

'Come on, come on, we must rush the place!'

'We've got 'em worried,' said Hammond, 'and there's someone in there who matters, Bill. Come on.'

'Wait a minute,' said Loftus. 'Wait a minute.'

He spoke in a low-pitched voice which did not carry to all of them. Davidson and Graham went forward, Webber with them. As they moved, a burst of revolver shooting came from the cottage, the shots sharp and clear, but the bullets hopelessly wide. Or so they thought, until Webber tripped up and went sprawling.

'Bill!' cried Hammond urgently.

'Who is it?' demanded Loftus tensely, looking towards the motor-cyclist. 'Who—Bruce, it's Pat Malone!'

In spite of his artificial leg he began to run down the hill towards Malone, who was no more than a hundred yards away, his engine snorting. Now that he was nearer they could see the blood on his forehead, and it seemed to them that his hands, on the handlebars, were also covered with blood. He was shouting, they saw his mouth opening but his words were drowned by the staccato beat of the engine.

The others were nearing the cottage, going cautiously along on their hands and knees. Two more bombs were flung at them, and the shooting came regularly.

Then vaguely Malone's voice reached Loftus.

'*Get away,*' he called, 'get away from there, get away!'

'What's that?' snapped Hammond.

'Get away,' said Loftus sharply, and then swung round and bellowed at the top of his voice: 'Graham—Wally—get back! Bruce, bring them back, for God's sake bring them back, I can't make it!'

Hammond stared at him, and then began to run.

The motor-cycle drew nearer. There was no longer any doubt that Malone was badly hurt, his face was deathly pale where it was not smeared with blood. He came up at high speed, and drew level with Loftus. His eyes were glittering and he was gasping for breath.

'Get 'em away, Bill, it'll be blue murder! They've dyna-
mited the whole ridge.'

Loftus heard: the words did not convey their full meaning for some seconds, although he had been afraid of what
Malone would say. He saw the Irishman stagger, but there
was no time to help him as he seized the motor-cycle and
straddled it himself. Its engine was still running. He saw
Malone fall heavily to the ground, as he drove furiously
towards the cottage and the ridge covered with trees, seeing
Hammond still a long way from the advance guard of the
attackers, hearing bomb explosions and gunfire.

The noise was too loud for Hammond's shouts to reach
the men, and Loftus knew that only he could manage to save
them, by getting in front of them and sending them back.

The wind rushed past his forehead, he found breathing
difficult, and when he shouted as he drew nearer the words
did not seem to carry more than a few feet. He took the
cycle in a wide half-circle approaching the further end of
the cordon. He realised then that the attackers were taking
the business grimly, and meant to break through at all costs,
believing that the quicker the opposition was smashed the
better. But for Malone's warning there would have been an
echo of that in Loftus's mind, although even then he would
have thought that it was too easy.

Too easy——

He reached the end of the line of men, and yelled to
the nearest:

'Get back as far as you can. *Get—back!*'

One man heard and understood, and turned to run.
But the others were too intent on their task to see what was
happening, crawling grimly forward and firing as they went.
Loftus rode along the line, between two fires. Once a Mills
bomb went over his head and pitched behind the men: the

blast from the explosion unsteadied him, but did not make him lose his balance. He noticed in a queer, detached way that the Mills bomb dropped into a crater made by an earlier one; there were three craters, lined up and not twenty feet away from one another.

He reached the next man and shouted the same order, then went on. Man after man turned back, bent low in retreat, to keep out of the revolver fire coming from the house. Loftus did not need to go to the far end of the line, for the last three men saw what the others were doing and followed their example.

Loftus looked towards the cottage.

The temptation to go on and explore was great, but he drew a deep breath abruptly, for he could see a movement inside one of the rooms. It was a shadow at first, showing a queer mechanical movement; and then a Mills bomb was lobbed out of the window *by a mechanical arm.*

'There's no one there,' he thought oddly.

He stopped the motor-cycle. He looked at the cottage, and then heard his name being called by Davidson and the others. He kicked off again, and as the engine roared, turned the machine towards the main group of men by the copse. By then, most of the others had reached it, and only a few seconds were needed for him to join them.

Then he heard the first rumble of an explosion.

# Chapter 21
# It Must Be Quayle

It was underground, a deep rumbling roar which shook the earth. He felt it shaking as he went along, and once was almost thrown. He kept his balance and pressed harder onwards, sending the machine racing towards the copse. The men there had flung themselves down, except for Hammond, who was gesticulating wildly and shouting to Loftus.

Loftus reached him.

He nearly fell off the cycle, which went over, and then straightened up. As he did so he heard another rumbling roar underground, and simultaneously saw a cloud of dirt and dust rise up some distance beyond the cottage. It was not an eruption with any spectacular effect; the earth subsided and trees disappeared, going downwards not upwards, in a tidy, almost orderly, fashion.

Downwards, not upwards.

Another roar followed, while Loftus stared at the cottage and saw it crumple, the walls falling inwards. *Then it disappeared,* although with no great billow of smoke or flame: it just sank out of sight, and the outlying trees, and shrubs, fences and small outbuildings went with it. The brown earth was sucked downward, and the men who were nearby could feel the trembling, hear the rumbling.

Another explosion, and the line of trees which covered the ridge disappeared, leaving no trace; their distance from the cottage was nearly a mile, thus the eeriness of their going, without wreckage or debris, was the greater. Where there had been solid earth and grass there was now nothing but a great void. Until that moment they could not see beyond the belt of trees, but as the gap appeared, the distant fields of the valley beyond, Heath Place, garish in its untouched solidity, was opened up to them. They could see, too, the cricket field which Brian Howe had pointed out to Mike.

For how long?

None knew for certain that the mining had not been carried underground to a spot beneath which they themselves were standing, but they watched, fascinated with the horror of it, as more and more gaps appeared in the trees, more and more great stretches of earth disappeared. Where there had been fields, hedges, mounds, hillocks, barns, gates, haystacks, cattle, and horses, there was nothing. Everything was swallowed by the craters, not one or two but a dozen of them, until the men were standing within thirty yards of the edge of the ridge instead of a mile away.

Dust and smoke were rising upwards, a great pall which spread over Lashley in a deepening cloud.

Loftus broke the vocal silence while the rumbling continued and flocks of birds rose high in the air, shrill cries declaring their fear and excitement, while in distant fields the cattle stampeded and the high-pitched whinneying of a horse reached their ears.

'I wonder if the village is all right?' said Loftus.

No one answered.

All of the party had withdrawn in time, and Webber limped towards them, his face set in a drawn expression, a little trickle of blood coming from a cut in his right cheek. He drew near to Loftus, and said:

'I caught my foot and fell.'

He stopped abruptly, and turned to face the devastation. The rumbling had ceased but dust and smoke were rising over the wide area where the ground had subsided. Bleak and bare, the sight which met his eyes was one of desolation, all the greater because it had been so lovely a short while before.

Webber tightened his lips, while Loftus went on:

'They had a gadget in the house, tossing the bombs. Probably the shooting was mechanical, too. The idea was to draw us on and then swallow us up.' He brushed a hand over his forehead, and his voice hardened. 'But what the devil are we doing here? Bruce, will you take some of the others and get down to the village? Wally, and you, Graham, take a party down to the big house on the plain—Heath Place. Just for the sake of it,' he added grimly. 'Best, keep three or four of the Home Guards, will you? We'll go with 'em to wherever Pat came from.'

'Who—who brought the warning?' asked Webber.

'One of our men who was watching Colonel Ratcliffe,' said Loftus grimly. 'I'm hoping that he'll remember just how much the Colonel knows about this.'

The first two parties started off without further question, while Loftus approached Pat Malone, who was sitting against a tree with a uniformed policeman bending solicitously over him. Malone's face remained pale except where it was bloodstained. There was a glint in his eyes and a twisted smile on his lips despite the pain that he obviously suffered.

'Well, Pat,' said Loftus quietly.

'Did you ever hear the old saying "Leave it to Loftus"?' demanded Malone, and there was a laugh in his voice. 'Good man, Bill, but I thought you'd left it too long.' He paused and gasped for breath, then went on quickly, and more soberly: 'It was Ratcliffe, but you'll have guessed that. I paid him closer attention than he liked, and we had a quarrel. Then the fool began to boast what he was going to do to you, said he had someone who would look after you all, and he talked about the whole of the workings being blown up. Then he locked a door on me, as if a locked door was ever able to keep an Irishman in!'

Behind that half-jocular commentary was a story of great courage and endurance, Loftus knew; but it was doubtful whether the Irishman would ever relate exactly what had happened. His report to Craigie would be brief and factual; he had escaped, and brought the message. That was all that mattered.

'So we're sure of Ratcliffe now,' said Loftus. 'Any news of Quayle?'

'What a head I've got! I 'phoned Craigie before I was knocked out, and he told me that Quayle was on his way down here; he got as far as Bath anyway.'

Loftus's eyes narrowed.

'Well, well, they're all coming. We'll keep more than a weather-eye open for Sir Edmund.' He paused, and then added: 'Is there anything you know about a man named Hanton, of Heath Place?'

'Devil a bit,' Malone assured him.

'And Rita Ainsworth wasn't mentioned?'

'She was not,' declared Malone. 'Ah, I can see an ambulance coming, Bill, and I can do with a rest.'

Loftus smiled but was thoughtful as he turned to Webber, who had sent a man for another car as well as the ambulance. Webber looked ghostly pale as he said quietly:

'I can hardly believe Ratcliffe is in this. And Hanton—surely Hanton can't be?'

'We'll find out,' said Loftus. 'Malone says that Ratcliffe knew someone else was around to get us nicely on the mine before it caved in. We haven't got 'em all yet. But, thanks be, Brian Howe's all right,' he added softly.

The ambulance drew up, and was followed by an old Buick. Loftus climbed in next to Webber, the others crowded into the back. Webber was driving, and Loftus peered again towards the devastation wrought by the mines, but was somewhat happier because the village had not suffered, according to the men who had come from it. A small stream of people was on the move up the hillside, coming to see the chaos but kept away by two policemen whom Webber left on duty.

There was a nagging anxiety in Loftus's mind.

Ratcliffe had left his house and gone elsewhere, presumably somewhere nearby. There was his evidence that someone else was working in the neighbourhood, the someone who had set the pretty trap which must have succeeded but for Malone's wild drive. While there remained a man in the organisation, Brian Howe was in danger; but Loftus thought that Howe's danger would last only until he had left the village, and it would not be long before he was on the way to London.

Afterwards——

Could Brian take his brother's place successfully? Could he convince Vichy and Berlin that he would bring reliable information again and again? Were there any members of the Lannigan-Smith organisation at large who could send a warning to Berlin?

The whole plan stood or fell on the complete success of Brian's impersonation of his brother, and the slightest whisper of suspicion about him would ensure failure.

What would that failure mean?

The death of Brian Howe; but that was a risk the naval officer would accept without question. There was little danger, now, of further genuine information getting out of the country, although while Quayle, and minor spies unknown to them, remained, there was always a chance. Loftus did not let himself brood too much on that, for it seemed clear that the organisation could not work again effectively. Most of it was smashed, and this quiet little village, its headquarters, would serve no further purpose. Odd, thought Loftus, that so much could have been planned and plotted in the tiny place, and that the knowledge of it would not have been discovered for some time but for Brian Howe's anger because of his brother's conscientious objection.

'Nonsense,' muttered Loftus *sotto voce*. 'Mike started that trail.'

'What's that?' asked Webber.

'Sorry,' said Loftus briefly. 'I was talking to myself.' He lapsed into silence again, and went on thinking: 'Yes, Mike started it, after Regina. But it shouldn't have been possible. It went far too smoothly.' He turned to Webber. 'What do you know of Hanton of Heath Place, Inspector?'

Webber pursed his lips.

'He's a reputable enough gentleman,' he said. 'He's "new" to the district, as residents go here—he came not long after the last war.'

'How did he make his money?' asked Loftus.

'Tinned food for the Forces,' said Webber briefly.

'H'm. Well, so did lots of others; I suppose we can't hold that against him. Do you know whether Sir Edmund Quayle ever visited him?'

'I couldn't be sure,' said Webber. 'Quayle did call on Ratcliffe from time to time. Ratcliffe,' he repeated under his breath, 'I can't believe that he's in this.'

'We're past that stage,' said Loftus quietly.

'Well, there's his house,' said Webber resignedly.

He turned the car into the drive of a small Georgian house set in charming grounds and, like most of the better houses in the district, built on the brow of a hill commanding an admirable view of the surrounding countryside. Loftus had no eye for panorama or trees, but he did have eyes for a small wisp of smoke curling from one of the windows at the side of the house.

A fire was starting there.

As Webber stopped the car, Loftus opened the door and jumped out, rushing as fast as his stiff leg would carry him towards the smoke. Webber and the police followed, with Best close behind them. The door of the house was closed, but the Home Guards battered at it with the butts of their rifles. As they did so the smoke increased in density, the acrid smell wafting down from the side of the house.

The door crashed in. Loftus went through, with Best just behind him, and Webber at their heels.

Loftus was thinking that someone had stayed long enough at the house to set fire to the papers, vital papers if he was to get full information. He felt a fierce anger with himself for having waited so long before coming here, for it seemed that the fire had only just started. The smell inside the hall was not pronounced, and there was no sign of smoke.

Webber and Best passed Loftus and rushed up the stairs. All of them appreciated the urgency of the occasion, and

Best was carrying an automatic in his right hand. They turned into a passage, out of Loftus's sight, and then Loftus heard the thudding on another door.

He reached the passage in time to see Webber disappearing into it, and to hear Best shout: 'Got you!'

A surge of hope raised Loftus's heart as he limped along, and then entered the room. But as he was entering he saw Best leaning against the wall, a hand at his chest, which oozed blood, his eyes glazed. He saw Webber by the window, leaning out, and he forced himself to ignore the Department Z men.

Webber fired from the window.

His gun had a silencer, only a faint sound reaching Loftus's ears. But he gained the window in time to see a man sprawling on to a grass lawn, a man whose head was holed with the bullet from Webber's gun. A Home Guard, left on duty outside, was hurrying forward.

Webber drew back.

'Ratcliffe was here,' he said. 'The fire—next room.' Loftus turned and followed Webber out, sparing only a glance for the mountainous Best, who had slumped to the floor in an oddly twisted position.

A policeman was in the passage.

'Look after him,' said Loftus, and jerked a thumb over his shoulder.

The man went to obey, while Loftus reached Webber, who was putting his full weight against the next door. Smoke was curling from the floor gap in thin wisps, and the smell was much stronger. The door shook and quivered under impact, and then broke down.

A volume of smoke made Loftus and Webber choke as they staggered through. Near the fireplace, on the carpet, was a mass of flames leaping two or three feet into the room. There were signs of disorder and confusion, papers were all about the floor and littered a large desk. The smoke was so thick that it was possible only to see halfway across the room, and Loftus looked about desperately for something to quench the flames. He had found nothing when two policemen arrived with fire extinguishers, and the fight started.

To Loftus it all seemed extraordinarily impersonal, as if he were acting compulsively and without choice or volition. Disjointed thoughts and scenes flashed through his mind. Ratcliffe had come back and fired the papers on learning of the failure of his plans. Best had broken into the room and been shot. Webber had shot and almost certainly killed Ratcliffe. But these were side issues, the papers were the things that mattered, and it seemed that they were being utterly destroyed. He watched the flames gradually dwindling, as the smoke increased and the unpleasant smell of the fire-extinguishing chemical became more insistent. He kept by the door, and after a while Webber joined him.

'There won't be a lot left,' said the Inspector.

'No. We're just a little too late for everything. But we've got Ratcliffe. That's something, I suppose. I'm going to Hanton's place,' he added abruptly. 'Come with me, will you? And let your men salvage what they can from this.'

'Do you need me there?' asked Webber.

'Badly,' said Loftus.

That the fire had started too soon for him was a bitter thought, and he wondered whether the men who had gone to the unknown Hanton's place would have any greater luck. True, there was no proof at all that Hanton was concerned in it, but he had to make as sure as he could that nothing else went wrong.

177

Then there was Quayle——

Quayle, suspected from the first but whom he had never seen, who had been watched for weeks by Department men and others but had not made a single slip, whose dignified portentousness remained a joke at the Ministry, who made his associates and subordinates hate him, who had the opportunity for co-ordinating the information passed on to Vichy.

It *must* be Quayle.

But there were others. Ratcliffe had talked of those who were preparing the trap for Loftus and the rest of the party, but even without Ratcliffe's outburst, it was obvious enough that there must be someone else in the vicinity. Who could it be? Rita Ainsworth was a possibility, just a possibility and no more. The devil of it was that he did not know everyone in the district. He was plunging on the man Hanton because he seemed as likely as anyone; but that was no method of working, it was not even following a hunch.

They drove through the village, passing the gates of Lady Beddiloe's house. Loftus thought fleetingly of that charming old lady, and her calm endurance throughout all that had happened, and then set thought of her aside and went on, with Webber driving, down a steep hill and then on a flat road towards Heath Place. The name of the big house of the tinned food manufacturer, who had made a fortune out of the last war, was justified, for the heathland about it was covered with heather, just then fading, while there were gorse bushes, some still showing a few yellow blooms, although most of them were dark green and flowerless.

Massive gates, upheld by pillars of Bath stone, stood at the entrance of the main drive to the house. A constable was standing outside, and saluted as they passed. The drive seemed inordinately long, but soon it was possible to see the big, red-brick house, which even twenty years had not mellowed.

Outside was the Lagonda, and another policeman.

There were voices coming from the hall, and as Loftus limped in with Webber at his side he heard Wally Davidson's low and drawling voice.

'Now come, no offence meant or intended. Grim times, you know, we must ask questions.'

'Questions be damned!' exclaimed a little, bald-headed man with a red face; his colour, Loftus judged, being mostly due to anger. 'I won't have young ruffians coming 'ere—here—and asking me a lot of dam' silly questions. That's flat. I'll have the police after you, and——'

The bald-headed man, presumably Hanton of Heath Place, running out of threats as the others arrived, turned and saw Webber, and pointed a fat, quivering finger towards him.

'Now then, Webber, send these fellas out of my 'ouse.' In his rage his aspirates failed him, a music-hall joke in which Loftus felt no amusement. 'Do I know this? Are my friends all right? I've never heard such a lot of nonsense!'

'I think you'll find that they have full authority to ask questions, sir,' said Webber thinly.

'Authority. Authority! Whose authority? Yours? I'll see that you're reported. Webber, I'll talk to the Chief Constable myself if you don't clear them out!' He was truculent, confident of his ability to send the visitors packing. He ignored Davidson, who looked faintly bored, and Young Graham, who was obviously not pleased. 'Ain't it bad enough to 'ave such a disaster without a lot o' flummery nonsense. See that 'ill? See it!' He took three steps to the door on short, podgy legs, and pointed across the parkland surrounding the house towards the scene of desolation, while wiping the perspiration from his neck and forehead. 'Look at it! All my land, all my——'

Loftus broke in sharply:

'Let's discuss that later, sir. Do you know Sir Edmund Quayle?'

He had no idea what questions Davidson and Graham had asked, and wanted only to break through Hanton's stream of pompous absurdities. He succeeded, for the little bald-headed man swung round on him, a fist clenching.

'What do you mean? Do I know Sir Edmund! Of *course* I know Sir Edmund, a better man there never was! I—why——'

He broke off abruptly.

Loftus turned to look out of the door, for another car came along the drive, and he saw Bruce Hammond at the wheel, with Mike Errol, Brian Howe, Regina and another woman with him in the car. The other woman was Rita Ainsworth, who was next to Bruce. As the car drew nearer Hanton peered short-sightedly towards it. His colour faded; he half-turned and would have made for the stairs had Loftus not stretched out a hand and gripped his arm.

'Let me go!' snapped Hanton. 'Let me go!'

'Shortly,' said Loftus quietly. 'We'll see what this is about first.'

He felt the man trembling under his grip as the carload of people climbed out, Bruce Hammond and Rita in the lead. They hurried into the house, and as they came Rita cried:

'That's him, that's him!'

'Who?' asked Loftus, forcing himself to keep a grip on the situation, bewildered by the woman's manner, but keeping Hanton in a tight hold. 'Who, Mrs. Ainsworth?'

'The man who was always at Queen Street,' shouted Rita, 'the man who was always giving Lannigan orders. That's him, *Hanton!*'

'Well, well,' said Loftus. 'We are having a time.'

'I—I don't know what she's talking about,' gasped Hanton. 'Who's Lannigan? Who——'

'You know who he is!' Rita shrieked at him. 'He's the man you paid to kill my husband. You've always hated me, ever since I married Martin you've always hated me!' She swung round on Loftus and went on in the same high-pitched voice: 'He used to pretend to be a friend of mine, a fine friend he was. *He wanted to marry me.* My father wanted me to marry him, too, the pair of them thought I'd do what I was told, but they were wrong, damn them, I left home and I haven't seen them since, except when Hanton's come to Queen Street!'

'I—I don't know what she's talking about,' mumbled Hanton. 'Silly little chit, lot of nonsense. I—I don't know her.' He turned to Webber. 'Inspector, you——'

'Don't know me!' screamed Rita. 'You double-crossing liar, you know me all right! You know my father, too, and I know what you've been doing now. If you'd let Martin alone I wouldn't have told on you, but I'll tell them everything I know, everything!'

'Shut up!' Hanton shouted at her.

'Don't you think——' began Webber, to be cut short by Loftus's quiet:

'Just a moment, Inspector. Mrs. Ainsworth, who is your father?'

'Don't you even know that?' The woman looked at him contemptuously. 'Sir Edmund Quayle, of course; when I married Martin he disowned me. But that didn't matter, even if I left him I loved Martin, I——' She stopped, looking sharply from Loftus to Webber.

She opened her lips, but before she spoke Webber suddenly kicked out at Loftus, and sprinted to the door.

'Stop him, stop him!' screamed Rita. '*He was at Queen Street too!*'

# Chapter 22

# An Englishman Goes North

It was Wally Davidson, so lethargic of appearance and slow of movement, who first drew his gun from his pocket and fired at Webber's legs. He hit the policeman, who pitched down the few steps of the porch, tried to get up, then snatched at a gun in his pocket. With the same easy speed Davidson fired and struck Webber's wrist. Webber gasped and fell back, while Hanton turned and ran towards the stairs.

'I don't think,' said Young Graham.

He caught the man without difficulty, grasping him by the scruff of the neck and leading him back to the centre of the hall. Loftus had picked himself up, with Bruce's help, while Davidson and two Home Guards were bending over Webber.

Loftus drew a deep breath.

'Of course, Webber,' he said like a man in a dream. 'I'd missed him completely. O.C. police around here. Suspicious characters frequently at the cottage, a cottage owned by a conchie and a suspect. Couldn't "believe" it of Ratcliffe, couldn't he?' He paused and then went on in the same dazed voice: 'Ratcliffe was quite right, you led us on, Webber. You fell down pretending you were hit before the rush on the cottage started. That should have told me. Then you got to Ratcliffe's house first. My God, it was you who shot Best, and then Ratcliffe—Ratcliffe, to stop him from talking. Best, because he suddenly suspected you.'

Webber glared at him, but said nothing.

Loftus turned to Rita Ainsworth, but before she spoke Bruce Hammond said quietly:

'I found that she didn't know of her husband's death, Bill. She was pretty worked up about it, and I asked a few questions. She knew something was brewing, knew her father and Hanton were in some rogue's game together. Presumably that's why Hanton wanted to marry her, to keep it all in the family. When she married Ainsworth it really started the trouble between Ainsworth and Quayle. She told me that Hanton had been to Queen Street quite often.'

The girl was standing by the wall, and Regina, who had not spoken, had an arm about her. Loftus brushed his hair back from his forehead, looked at them both, and then turned to Hanton.

'We've things to talk about,' he said. 'Before that, we'll get Quayle under lock and key. Bruce, will you——'

The bald-headed little food manufacturer stood back a pace. He was still trembling, but there was an odd dignity about him as he looked at Loftus and spoke.

'You don't have to worry about Quayle. He was getting nervous, so he's gone. He was blown up in the mine, and the other fools with him.'

Loftus drew a sharp breath.

'Is that the truth?'

'It's the truth,' Hanton assured him. 'Quayle knew you were watching him, and he got too nervous, nerves don't pay in a thing like this. I'm beaten now, and I'll admit it. *I've* arranged this thing, Loftus, and I've been watching you working against me. I didn't think you'd win,' he said simply, 'but it got too complicated. Ainsworth went off the deep end, and we thought he knew something we had to find out. That started it. Then you got busy on Lannigan and Smith, the poor fools.'

Loftus said slowly: 'They worked for Berlin.'

Hanton shrugged his plump shoulders.

'So what? I didn't. I worked for myself. So did Quayle and others. Quayle got the dope, I fixed it to be sent out from here, had a transmitter in the mine that could get anywhere, and no one could find it. Had it blown up because I thought I could still make it. I'd forgotten Rita.' He looked at the woman dispassionately, and then went on: 'Wondering why it didn't come out that she was Quayle's daughter, aren't you? That's easy—she had five thousand a year allowance provided she kept quiet about it. Ainsworth knew it, and tried to blackmail Quayle. Poor sap, he hadn't any guts, couldn't even do that properly.'

'But why?' demanded Loftus.

Hanton gave a quick, sardonic smile.

'Ask yourself. Quayle's been married fifteen years, and Rita's twenty-seven, even if she doesn't look it.' He shrugged his shoulders. 'I got her in with Lannigan so that he could watch her, and she thought she was watching her father. I pretended to be doing a deal with Lannigan, he didn't know that Quayle and me were as close as that.' He held up two fingers, tightly set together. 'I had Lannigan and Smith *and* Berlin nicely foxed, Loftus. I sold out to Vichy for a big price, but I wouldn't deal direct with the Boche, that would have been asking for trouble. I had a pretty good crowd working,' he added detachedly. 'Teddy Howe needed money badly, and Webber was in the same boat, with both of them knowing about the old workings. I had Ratcliffe with me to draw you off if you got as far as Lashley. I'd forgotten Rita,' he added softly, 'as soon as I knew Ainsworth hadn't much on us, I forgot Rita. That was a mistake. I nearly left the other woman too late, too—Regina Brent, I mean.' He paused, and looked steadily at Loftus.

'Why were you after Brent's papers?' demanded Loftus.

'That's easy,' said Hanton. 'Quayle thought Brent had some damning stuff on him, and I fixed the accident in which Brent was killed. The papers we looked at last year didn't give us what we wanted, so we put them back. But when you fellows started watching Quayle he got nervous, so I had another attempt to get at the papers. Anything else you want to know?'

'Yes,' said Loftus. 'How did the messages get to Vichy?'

'You're not so good after all,' said Hanton. 'We had a transmitter in the mine, and Teddy Howe went over to collect the cash. You won't get Teddy, he'll be an English refugee in France!'

Loftus put his head on one side and regarded the little man. He felt a great sense of elation, for he had no doubt that he had heard the truth, and did not question the prospects of Brian Howe succeeding in the coming mission.

'So you didn't know that Edward Howe was dead,' he said softly. 'The team-work wasn't very good, because Webber knew.'

Hanton drew up to his full height, a little over five feet, and peered at Webber, who was sitting against the wall with rough bandages about his wrist and leg.

'Teddy's *dead*? And that two-timing twister didn't tell me?' Hanton stared at Loftus, then threw his head back and laughed, a high-pitched hysterical laugh, which showed more than anything else the degree of strain under which the man was labouring. '*Teddy's dead!* Webber didn't tell me. Of course, he knew we couldn't collect without Teddy, and I wouldn't pay out unless the cash came from France. I thought I had him where I wanted him, but he double-crossed me. If I'd known Teddy was dead I would have been away from here forty-eight hours ago.'

The man stopped, thrust his hands into his pockets, looked at Webber expressionlessly, and then shrugged. He did not speak again, even when he was led out of the room.

The elation of the party of Department Z agents, and those with them, was tempered by the news, learned soon after they had left Heath Place, that Best had died from his wound.

Webber had confessed to shooting him, and had admitted all the charges: like Hanton, he saw no point in maintaining any other attitude. There was proof, too, that Quayle was dead; he had been near one of the mine-shafts just before the explosion, and by some freak blast had been flung clear so that, although he had been killed outright, his features were quite recognisable.

For some time the thought of Best's death, and the knowledge that not once until the final act had Quayle been seen in the open, and then only casually, had weighed on Loftus's mind. He admitted to himself (and later to Hershall and Craigie) that there had been far more luck than he liked about the affair; but that did not matter, since they had the results.

And they had Brian Howe.

Loftus was in the back seat of the Lagonda with Brian, while Hammond, Davidson and Graham crowded in front. Rita Ainsworth was staying for the time being with Regina at Beddiloe House. Mike Errol, Cartwright, the Ministry of Mines expert, and several other agents who had followed Quayle from London that day were packed in another car behind Loftus's. Before they had left Lashley, an inquiry at the nearest hospital, where Webber and Pat Malone had been taken, earned the information that both men were 'doing well'.

Hanton was under arrest at his own house, where he was assisting the police—under a superintendent sent out from the regional headquarters—to go through his papers.

Hammond, at the wheel, pulled up at Loftus's Brook Street flat, and the two car-loads emptied. Three plain-clothes policemen were on duty outside the flats, and Loftus smiled a little at that, the only outward sign that Hershall was nearby.

Craigie, who had been forewarned by telephone, was waiting at the flat when the party went in. He gripped Loftus's hand warmly.

'Don't congratulate me,' said Loftus. 'The others have been showing me things. Where's the P.M.?'

'Waiting for you,' said Craigie. 'And Howe——' he looked at Brian Howe as Loftus introduced them, and then added: 'The Admiralty has released you for special service, and I gather from Loftus that you're willing to do what you can.'

'I'm willing all right,' said Brian Howe quietly.

'Good man,' said Craigie. 'Bill, will you come in next door with Bruce and Howe? The rest of you——' he paused, and smiled a little, not so much at the disappointment evident on the faces of some of them because they were not to be present at the interview with Hershall, but at Wally Davidson, who was opening a cabinet and removing two bottles.

'We'll be all right,' said Davidson with a drawl. 'Go to it, soldier!'

Loftus, Hammond, Howe and Craigie went through the secret doorway connecting the two flats. It took them through a narrow passage and then into a comfortably furnished lounge. In there was Hershall and two secretaries, the secretaries perspiring freely, both in their shirt-sleeves.

Hershall was dictating, but broke off when the others entered. His round, pale face was enlivened, his eyes were gleaming, the innate forcefulness of the man had never shown to better advantage. He pushed his chair back, waved the secretaries away, and then looked at Loftus with a half-smile.

'Incredible fellow, Loftus! You've managed it again.'

Loftus raised an eyebrow.

'The others did it for me, and I won't go into the way the luck ran, sir.'

'Luck be damned!' exclaimed Hershall. 'You worked for it. Can't be sure which way things will turn, you never can. I only wish you could guarantee anything, but—oh, never mind that, now.' His eyes turned towards Brian Howe, who was standing stiffly to attention. His gaze lingered for some seconds, and then he said quietly: 'Sit down, gentlemen. Now, Mr. Howe, you know what we're asking of you?'

'I do, sir.'

'You've no reservations about accepting?'

'None at all, sir.'

'I'll go over some of the ground again,' said Hershall, and took a cheroot from a case in his pocket. Loftus struck a match and Hershall leaned forward, drew on the cheroot, grunted his thanks and then went on: 'You will go to Vichy and meet a man at an address Loftus will give you.

Before you go, radio transmission of certain information will be broadcast for your contact man to pick up. You will reinforce that radio statement with information of an impending large scale invasion of the Continent and the assurance that you can give full details of it at a given time. Is that all clear?'

'Perfectly clear, sir.'

'You will have with you carefully prepared details of the "organisation" of which you are supposed to be a member—Craigie has been working that out for you. It will stand up to any investigation that the Germans can make over here, and I know of no one—and I speak from what Loftus and Craigie tell me—who can discredit your story, or distinguish between you and your brother.'

'I see, sir,' said Brian quietly.

'You will return from France by a small motor launch used, we understand, by your brother. That part of the organisation has not been disturbed. You will report the success of your mission to agents who will contact you, and then you will take back to Vichy—or Berlin, as you may be summoned there—full details of the coming invasion. That invasion plan will, of course, be a false one. You don't need to be told the implications of that, nor to realise that much of the success of our real attack depends on you.'

'I don't, sir,' said Brian mechanically.

'Any failure will possibly lengthen operations by six months or more,' said Hershall. 'I am being fully frank with you, Mr. Howe. You deserve that frankness.'

'And I appreciate it, sir,' said Brian. 'I don't feel that anything less can—can—make full retribution for my family's treachery.' His lips were set when he finished, but he looked squarely into Hershall's eyes.

Hershall said quietly: 'If you do this successfully, Howe, you will have done far more than that. As I see it, but for your brother's misdemeanours, the opportunity would never have been vouchsafed us. Good out of evil.' He raised his eyebrows, and smiled a little. 'I have every confidence in you, and I hope I shall see you again afterwards. Be sure that full recognition will be made, in any event, and be sure also that the faith and trust of the country, as well as myself, are with you.'

Howe's eyes were suspiciously bright.

'Thank you, sir.'

'Good,' said Hershall briskly. 'Good. Look after him well, Loftus. Who will be going to Vichy after him?'

'Hammond and some of the others,' said Loftus, 'and there are plenty over there. I don't think anything will go seriously wrong, sir.' He hesitated, and Hershall snapped: 'Well?'

'Are you staying here much longer?' asked Loftus.

Hershall looked at the end of his cheroot, and his lips curved before he chuckled.

'No, Loftus, only an hour or two. I'm broadcasting at half-past eleven. A shock for the Boche, eh?' He chuckled again, but then his face grew sombre, and he added very softly: 'Not such a shock as he's going to get, I think.'

Brian saluted, and turned to go. Loftus went with him. Hershall stared at the door as it closed, drew on his cheroot, cleared his throat, and then said gruffly:

'Amazing war, Craigie. Never known so much depend on individuals. A war of machines, we call it. We'd be in a bad way if that were all. Well, I've got to get busy, I mustn't be fuddled at the microphone tonight!'

He pressed a bell, and the secretaries returned. He nodded and smiled to Craigie, who went out and joined the others.

Brian Howe had gone with Loftus, but Craigie gave the party a résumé of what had happened. Finally, he told them that Hershall was to broadcast.

Over the radio throughout the land the news was being given out at ten minute intervals. '*Listeners are reminded that the Prime Minister will be speaking at eleven-thirty tonight in both Home and Forces wave lengths.*' It was given out in the middle of dance programmes, in the midst of a play, several times during a symphony concert and as often during a variety programme. It reached the homes of England, the public houses, the cinemas and the theatres. It was carried from hand to mouth, the neighbours rushing from their hearths to make sure that it had been heard next door. It was shouted on buses and trams, trains and taxis, it was cried jubilantly in the streets. There was no second when the name of Hershall was not on a thousand lips, no face which had not brightened at this complete scotching of rumour. From a steady resistance against the depression that rumour had created, there grew a wave of elation like nothing that had ever happened in the country, from the beginning of war.

It spread like wildfire, bringing cheers and shouting, and dancing and singing. It was announced from the footlights and from screens, it set the populace talking and humming and buzzing with the news; it breathed new life into the old and the young, the tired and the disheartened.

Eleven o'clock came; eleven-fifteen.

There were few receiving sets in the land not tuned in at twenty-five past eleven, and faces grew tense as the minutes went by. Then at eleven-thirty precisely Hershall was on the air; and over the land there was a breathless hush as his clear, deliberate voice greeted them.

He began:

'They thought they had killed me, my friends, but they were wrong, and I am here. I have not a long message for you tonight, I will not remind you again of what has happened in the past, nor what is happening now. I need not recount stories of the enormous forces of our aircraft which deliver terror to the Nazi people each night and every night, I need not tell you that Germany is already reeling under our blows.

'But you have been waiting for other news.

'You have asked for "*attack*", land attack.

'And such an attack there will be, before very long, a blow such as Hitler cannot withstand, a devastating blow which will send his armies back, armies already weakened by hardship and lack of support from the Home Front. Already they are reeling under the blows from Russia, mighty blows which are gaining weight; and tonight I send a message to our Russian allies, and to the Americans who are with us and will fight with us. The day is approaching. We will and shall attack, and we shall win. I have never prophesied before, but I prophesy now: we shall set foot on the Continent, and we will not be driven back. Whether the final victory will come in weeks or months I cannot tell. I do not think that it will take years.

'You have asked for an offensive, you have worked and fought for it, and to every man and woman and child some part of the preparations are due, no one need think that he or she is doing nothing. You have played your part gloriously, and you will continue to do so while the Army and the Navy and the Air Force does its work.

'Be of great heart, for the hour is approaching.'

He stopped: there was a long pause before another voice came to the microphone. In that pause there was hardly a voice raised in Great Britain. Men and women and children eyed one another, echoing the glorious confidence of the speech that they had prayed to hear. In some eyes there were tears, but in all hearts there was a great resurgence of hope.

In Regina Brent's and Lady Beddiloe's, at Lashley.

In the agents' at Loftus's flat, gathered about the microphone; Loftus was back with them, but Howe had left for Vichy, and Hammond soon after him.

Soon the news was being sent to the Continent, a Continent waiting to rise to strike and to help. Over the land of Europe and further afield there was the great upsurge of belief in victory, *early* victory.

In Vichy, Brian Howe met the man who had last seen his brother, a man who had already been told that the news of the big plan for invasion had leaked out. From Vichy Howe went to Berlin, from Berlin, after a nightmare stay, he returned to Vichy and thence to England. He was burning with the desire to take his task through successfully, while the whole of Craigie's department were waiting or working, on tenterhooks for the great day. Many were in the occupied countries, many in Germany, preparing the enslaved peoples for the blow they would strike to help their own deliverance.

Few knew of Brian Howe's lone task.

Few knew that he reported the success of his first visit, but Loftus, Craigie and Mike Errol knew, knowing also that in England Howe was shadowed by Nazi agents but obtained the 'information' through a contact the Nazis could not connect with the Department or the Government. They knew, too, that he went back with the information for the location of the attack; and then reports came through that the Nazis were massing their men by night to counter it.

The people waited, with Hershall's message still alive in their hearts. A matter of weeks, they said, or days——Attack!

It came so swiftly that even the people whose hearts and lives were dedicated to that hour were taken by surprise. It came with a ferocity which made the Germans gasp in dismay. It went on furiously, with the Nazis fighting their desperate battle, the battle which might last for weeks or months but could have only one end.

If there is a sorrowful thing in the hearts of Loftus and Mike Errol, Craigie, Hammond and the other agents, it is that no news ever came from Brian Howe after his signal that the 'plans' had been delivered.

Waiting for trial the men who began the great betrayal heard news of the onslaught. In Lashley, Regina stayed with Aunt Bess, hearing from Mike by letter or telephone. In Guildford Hospital Mark Errol improved day by day, bemoaning the fact that he saw so little of the action, while marvelling at the speed with which Mike and Regina had come to an understanding.

To his nurse he declared, on hearing the news of their engagement, that two goldfish never could be satisfactorily divided among three people.

# NO DARKER CRIME

JOHN CREASEY

# CHAPTER 1
## 'SOMETHING OF INTEREST'

*Dear Mr. Garth,*

*If you will call at The Elms, Brookside Road, Wimbledon, about 7 p.m. today, you will hear something which I am sure will interest you greatly.*

There was no signature to the note. Nor was there any address. But the postmark was 'Wimbledon' and David Garth assumed it had been sent from The Elms. He drew his almost flaxen eyebrows together as he tried to recollect any acquaintance in Wimbledon—and to imagine what the matter of interest might be. His face, too long in the chin and nose to be quite handsome, cleared as he decided that it was of no importance. Dropping it on to the table, he lit a cigarette and glanced at his watch.

'Five to five,' he mused. 'I wonder if it's any use looking up Anne?'

He eyed the telephone in the corner of the long, narrow room, which was furnished with a variety of oddments inherited or acquired on his travels. A court cupboard in lovely, mellowed walnut, a Chippendale tripod table, two slung-chairs, their sound leather seats barely marked after two hundred years of usage, a beautiful gate-leg table, and, flanking the fire-place, two vast and very comfortable hide armchairs. A shaft of Autumn sunlight threw into bold relief the delicate inlay-work of a walnut Regency bookcase.

It would be pleasant to see Anne again, he reflected although now that she was engaged she might feel it would be indiscreet to meet him. His long, sensitive lips curved; without more ado he stepped to the telephone and dialled a Chelsea number.

The voice that answered made his heart leap, although he had believed himself quite cured of his infatuation for Anne Duval. 'I'll give you three guesses,' he told her.

She did not recognise him; or perhaps affected not to.

'Who did you say ...?'

'It's David,' he said, shortly. 'I wondered if ...'

'David!' she exclaimed. 'David, I ...'

There was a hint of excitement in her voice. Then she paused and her tone became flat and indifferent. But she carried it too far when she concluded: 'Oh, you mean David Garth? Hallo, David.'

'No, that's too bad!' he protested, not entirely joking. 'Once we were as one, but now you have the nerve to pretend you can mistake me for same other David. Anne, are you doing anything tonight?'

'I'm afraid so,' she said, a little too promptly. 'I've a dinner appointment. I'm terribly busy, these days, David—war work, you know.' She spoke quickly, as if to prevent him from interrupting. 'And the fact is, I *have* met several other Davids, recently—George knew them. Have you seen George, lately?'

'Does he respect the laws of ministerial discretion enough to forget to tell you I've been to America?' demanded Garth. 'Anyway, since it's been in most of the papers and on the radio ...'

'I don't get much chance to read the papers, these days,' she told him. 'Did you have a good journey?'

'Not a U-boat either way. Thanks for asking.'

'Oh, that's all right,' said Anne.

That startled him more than anything else. The Anne he had known so well would have seized on that note of raillery and snapped back some witty rejoinder and they would have laughed together. That was one of his pleasantest memories of Anne Duval—the ease of laughing with her. After their estrangement and her engagement to the more solid—and stolid—George, he had often reproached himself because he had taken Anne, and life, too lightly.

'I do wish I were free,' she added, after the slightest of pauses. 'Perhaps if you ring again—in about a week, say—I'll have an hour or two to spare. Sorry—I can't stop now. Goodbye, David!'

He replaced the receiver with mixed feelings.

That evasive, contradictory reaction was so unexpected from Anne. It contrasted not only with his memories of her, but also with that first eager 'David!' It was as if she had allowed her feelings free rein, then suddenly regretted it.

'The truth is,' he reflected wryly, 'she thinks I might be too disruptive an influence, so she's playing safe. I've received my *congé* and that's that. The question is what to do with the evening?'

He glanced at the note again, with a mild stirring of curiosity. It was written in a bold, flowing hand, with green ink on mauve paper. The over-all effect was flamboyant.

Undecided still, he dropped the letter on to the table again, and wandered across to a small bureau near the window. The writing flap was down and there was a pile of newspaper cuttings on it.

In the sunlight, his blond hair was creamy gold. His eyes—blue, dark-fringed, wide-set and deceptively sleepy-looking—scanned the top cutting. It was from the *New York Daily Mirror* and it had a headline an inch deep:

## GARTH SAYS NOW OR NEVER
*English Spokesman Rates U.S.A.*

'David Garth, dreamy-eyed, handsome, lazy-looking, belied his appearance and put pep into his speech at Ligham Hall last night. Question—does Garth, from Ministry of Propaganda, Whitehall, speak for himself or for the British Government? If for himself, one day he will be caught with his pants down. But Garth is nobody's fool. Internal quarrels and isolationist U.S.A. outlook, he said, will only lead to another world war. Others have said the same but not with such vigor and feeling. Don't be taken in by his pretty blue eyes. Garth's dynamite. Maybe we need some.'

Garth smiled briefly and looked at the next cutting from the *New York Times:*

*David Garth Speaks for Himself*
*Not Views of Whitehall, He Says*

'Asked by a *Times* reporter whether his speech at Ligham Hall should be regarded as official, David Garth said NO in Capital letters. We question the wisdom of permitting official spokesmen to make unofficial pronouncements in public.'

He picked up another, from the London *Daily Telegraph:*

## Mr. David Garth To Return
### Lecture Tour Cut Short

'It is understood that Mr. David Garth, distinguished critic and, more lately, lecturer for the Ministry of Propaganda, is to return from the United States, where some of his recent speeches have caused some misunderstanding. Mr. Garth's return is for private reasons and it is hoped that he will be able to return to the United States before the year is out.'

Garth shrugged, dropped the cutting, and turned to gaze out of the window into Jermyn Street.

He was sardonically amused by this evidence of the delicacy of the panjandrums in Whitehall—while appreciating the fact that an official reproof, sharply delivered to him personally had not been made public.

Actually, he had been recalled for speaking too bluntly; but secretly, he had a shrewd idea that some of his superiors applauded his plain speaking. Yet that did not excuse him for using his position to make statements which might arouse ill-feeling.

'Still, as a private citizen, I wouldn't have gone over at all,' he mused. 'I wonder if they'll let me resign?'

He knew it was much more likely that he would be sent on a lecture tour in England, with careful instructions on what not to say. They might have released him for the Army, but a motoring accident had left him with a stiff left arm and he had been rated Grade 3 since his 'medical', two years earlier.

The telephone startled him.

He went across and lifted the receiver.

'David Garth speaking.'

A man spoke. A stranger to him, his voice quiet, but with a note of authority; a voice which commanded immediate respect.

'Good-evening, Mr. Garth. You won't know me, but I must ask your indulgence in a matter which you may find somewhat startling.'

'I say, who …?'

'Before you ask any questions, Mr. Garth, would you mind telling me: have you received an invitation, unsigned, to visit a house of which you have never heard?'

'Good Lord!' exclaimed Garth, amazed.

'Then you have?' The voice held evident satisfaction. 'Mr. Garth, there is no time now for explanations, but I will be greatly obliged if you will go to the Regent Palace Hotel lounge at once. There, you will be met and given some explanation of this unusual request.'

'But …'

'You might find in this an opportunity for re-establishing your reputation at the M.O.P.', went on the other, drily. 'On the other hand, you might find an outlet for even more direct self-expression! Don't ignore this request, will you?'

The line went dead while Garth was still seeking an effective reply. Frowning, he replaced the receiver, lit a cigarette and took the note from the table again. As he read it, the unknown caller's message ran through his mind.

He had to admit it had been cleverly phrased. He was feeling pretty sore about his recall and the probability that for some time to come he would be closely watched, and all his speeches scrutinised for any departure from the orthodox. Now, he had been offered two alternatives—vague ones, it was true, yet with possibilities. Moreover, the speaker had implied that he had some official connection, perhaps with the M.O.P. itself....

He read the note again, slowly:

*Dear Mr. Garth,*
 *If you will call at The Elms, Brookside Road, Wimbledon, about 7 p.m. today, you will hear something which I am sure will interest you greatly.*

It was half past five, and he had nothing else arranged. A visit to the Regent Palace, only a few hundred yards away, would at least do no harm, he decided.

He walked through to Piccadilly and along to the hotel, entered the crowded foyer through the revolving doors, and approached the lounge.

There were few more popular meeting-places in the centre of London, and a hum of conversation filled the large, ornately-ceilinged room. Several women sitting alone eyed his tall figure, immaculate in dark-blue hopsack, with unconcealed interest. But no one made any deliberate move to attract his attention.

Frowning, Garth looked about him, wondering how he could be identified amongst so many. And even if he were, he thought, it would surely be impossible to talk without being overheard. He strolled the length of the wide passage between the massed chairs and sofas, alert for anyone who might seem to be regarding him with especial interest.

No one approached him.

He retraced his steps as far as the lounge doorway, beginning to wonder whether he could possibly be the victim of some hoaxer. A waitress passed him and handed a note to a hall-porter, and a moment later, the man came over to him.

'Excuse me, sir—would you be Mr. Garth?'

'I am,' Garth said,

'Your friend's sent a message, sir, to say he's sorry he can't get down to see you, but will you be good enough to go to Room 316? That's on the third floor, sir ...'

He broke off, as he was button-holed by a vociferous middle-aged woman plaintively demanding that he find her a seat, and Garth nodded and strode off towards the lifts. Up on the third floor, he followed the deserted corridors until he reached the door of 316; then, for the first time, doubtful of the wisdom of going further, he paused and reached for his cigarettes as he considered.

He was just about to light one, when a man turned the corner. Tall and well-built, he wore a Savile Row suit with a casual elegance that matched Garth's own. He looked somewhere about thirty-five and was clearly in the pink of condition. His face creased into an engaging smile as he drew up.

'I've beaten you to it, then?' he said, cheerfully. 'Don't look dumbstruck, old chap—we're quite harmless!' And gripping Garth's right arm, he turned the handle of the door and pushed it open.

Propelled into the room, Garth stared confusedly at a man on the bed.

It was as if the man from the passage had contrived to pass him, take off his coat, and lain down on one of the beds. But the grip on his arm remained firm until the door was closed.

'It's all right,' he assured Garth, as the man on the bed laconically raised himself and swung his feet to the floor. 'We're two separate people. And we're not even brothers ...'

'Which is no cause for regret,' remarked the second man. 'We are ...'

'Cousins,' supplied the first. 'It's always quicker to get it over this way, I think. Look carefully and you will see the subtle difference. My hair is a shade lighter ...'

'Only it has more oil upon it,' quoth the man on the bed. 'My eyes are darker, too.'

'Oh, yes?' murmured Garth, glancing from one to the other as they eyed him expectantly. Then he realised how futile the comment must have sounded. But he *felt* futile. With other men who acted so outrageously he might have felt annoyed, yet there was an engaging good humour about this couple which invited reciprocity. He made the effort:

'I suppose I haven't strayed into an asylum?' he asked, drily.

The man on the bed beamed approval.

'No asylum.' He spoke more quickly and crisply than his cousin: 'Some would say that such should be our lot, but Fate is kind ... Everything all right, Mark?'

'Yes,' added the other. 'He wasn't followed—neither was I. The trouble with us,' he added, to Garth, 'is that we have suspicious minds. In the simplest things, we see great possibilities for evil.' He grinned. 'No, don't say it! We're going to explain, partly, at least. Sit down and light that cigarette and make yourself at home.'

He indicated the only easy-chair in the small room, and Garth crossed to it and seated himself with a good-humoured shrug.

He was a pretty good judge of men. And the one thing obvious to him, about this pair, was that their facetious back-chat was only a façade. And men of the calibre he sensed them to be would not have gone to such trouble to get him here and meet him unseen, without some very good reason.

Their precautions against being seen with him, indeed—while undeniably quickening his interest—gave him a feeling of faint disquiet. He waited with mounting curiosity as the second man seated himself on the upright chair near the bedside telephone. Then the man on the bed announced, solemnly:

'I will now unfold the mystery.'

'Never mind the mystery,' interrupted 'Mark'. 'Get to the point!'

'What, put the cart before the horse?' protested the other. Then grinned again, as he added: 'Although I agree—Garth will probably start throwing his weight about, if we don't start somewhere. The point first, then. We want you to go to Wimbledon tonight, Garth, but not as a free agent. We want you to go as a representative of—er—a small department in Whitehall, to which we have the honour to belong.' More seriously, he concluded: 'If you're convinced that it's worth while, can you go?'

Garth hesitated before saying:

'Yes, but …'

'Ours the "buts"!' said the other, promptly. 'If you can go, and are convinced you should, will you still go when I tell you that the venture might hold more than a modicum of danger?'

# Want another perfect mystery?

# Get your next classic crime story for free...

Sign up to our Crime Classics newsletter where you can discover new Golden Age crime, receive exclusive content and never-before published short stories, all for FREE.

From the beloved greats of the Golden Age to the forgotten gems, best-kept-secrets, and brand new discoveries, we're devoted to classic crime.

If you sign up today, you'll get:

1. A free novel from our Classic Crime collection.
2. Exclusive insights into classic novels and their authors and the chance to get copies in advance of publication, and
3. The chance to win exclusive prizes in regular competitions.

Interested? It takes less than a minute to sign up. You can get your novel and your first newsletter by signing up on our website www.crimeclassics.co.uk

Made in the USA
Middletown, DE
14 November 2022

15000800R00128